ALANNAH

a slater brothers novella

NEW YORK TIMES & USA TODAY BESTSELLING AUTHOR

L. A. CASEY

Alannah
a slater brothers novella
Copyright © 2018 by L.A. Casey
Published by L.A. Casey
www.lacaseyauthor.com

Alannah / L.A. Casey – 1st ed.
ISBN-13: 978-1720356158 | ISBN-10: 1720356157

For Edel, who is the best soundboard.

TABLE OF CONTENTS

CHAPTER ONE

"**A**lannaaaahhh … I'm coming for you."

I spun around, my hair a mass of thick, dark waves flying after me. I looked from my left to my right, wondering where the echoed whisper was coming from. The voice that spoke was uncomfortably familiar to me, but I couldn't recall who it belonged to. All I knew was that fear caused my muscles to tighten, and my throat to run dry. My body was tense, and the hair on the nape of my neck stood at attention. Something was *very* wrong. I looked around once more, and it was only at that moment I realised that I couldn't remember walking into my office. I looked down at my body and blinked in surprise. I *definitely* couldn't remember putting on the beautiful white dress I was wearing. In fact, I couldn't remember when I purchased the dress in the first place.

"Damien?" I called out, confusion gripping me. "Where are ye'?"

"He's a little tied up at the moment, angel."

I shrieked when the voice spoke directly behind me, but when I turned to face the person, I was met with thin air. My body began to tremble, and silent sobs climbed their way up my throat. I jumped when I heard a clicking noise to my right. My lips parted with shock as I watched my easel set itself up without a person in sight to perform the action. I wanted to turn, to flee the room and never look back, but I couldn't. I was frozen to the spot as my eyes were locked on the impossible scene before me.

I sucked in a sharp breath when I blinked, and suddenly, I was standing in front of my easel with a pencil in my hand. A large blank canvas was before me, and as if I was controlled by someone else, my arm rose, and my hand began to draw on the canvas. I whimpered with fright as I fought for control of my body, but I was completely at the mercy of whatever possessed me. I could do nothing but watch in horror as my hand drew an image at an unnatural speed. It wasn't just an image, though ... It was a sketched film.

I had drawn perfect likenesses of the Slater brothers, and when they began to move, smile, and turn to look at me, my heart just about beat out of my chest. I watched as their smiles turned to frowns, then as their frowns turned to pained expressions as cuts and tears appeared on their bodies. Thick, red liquid began to spill from the brothers, but then it wasn't just on the brothers anymore; it began to seep *through* the canvas. I watched as it slowly dripped down the sketch and splashed onto the floor, causing a puddle to form around my bare feet. The liquid splashed onto my white dress, decorating it in red.

The smell was heavy and metallic, and I knew it had to be blood.

"I think this is your best creation yet, angel."

I fell onto my behind when control of my body suddenly returned to me. It didn't hurt like I expected it to. In fact, I felt nothing at all. My breathing was laboured as a shadow fell over me, and apprehension flooded me. I looked up, and when my eyes landed on *him*, my lips parted, and my heart stopped.

"*Morgan?*"

Morgan Allen, who was really Carter Miles, smiled down at me, and his vibrant violet eyes seemed to twinkle in delirious amusement.

"Angel," he said, tilting his head to the side. "Oh, how I've missed you."

I furrowed my brows as I clumsily got to my feet and stumbled a few steps away from Morgan, putting some much-needed space between us.

"You can't be 'ere," I warned. "Ye' *promised* that ye'd go away and *stay* away."

"That was when you rejected the Slater brothers," he said with a wicked grin. "But you've made up with them … You've opened your heart to them once again, and I can't have that, angel. Not when they've killed people close to me. Murderers don't get a happily ever after, not in this story."

My knees knocked together and threatened to give way at any moment.

"Mor-Morgan," I stammered. "Ye' said ye'd never hurt anyone … D'ye remember that?"

"And *you* said you loved Damien and that you wanted to marry him and have his babies, but that's not true," he replied with a menacing snicker. "I guess we're *both* liars."

"I … I do want to marry Damien and have his children. I *do*."

"No, you don't," Morgan replied smugly. "I'm in your head, angel, remember? That means I know *everything* that goes on inside it. You *want* Damien, but you *don't* want his last name or his kids."

"No," I said, wrapping my arms around my waist. "No, that's *not* true."

"It's the fear in you," Morgan continued as he slowly began to circle me like a predator. "You said you wanted to marry him, to have his children … but when you thought about that, you realised you were too scared to make it a reality because what if you had his babies and they died? What if you married Damien and *he* died? Starting a life with him was too terrifying for you to consider. You're playing games with Damien, and you *know* he doesn't like games."

"Shut up!" I pleaded. "Shut up, shut up, *shut up!*"

"Oh, angel." He chuckled, the rumbling sound echoing around the room. "You're a little mouse in a big, bad world. Do you know what I am?"

I shook my head.

"The mouse *trap*."

I began to cry, the sobs wracking my body until I was a trembling mess of emotion.

"Ye' s-said ye'd n-never hu-hurt me."

"We have *both* said things we didn't mean … Isn't that right, *Lana*?"

I jumped about a foot into the air when a loud bang sounded from my left, and when I swung my attention in that direction, my knees finally gave out, and I dropped to them with a thud. Before me were the Slater brothers, all tied up, cut, and bloody … just like they were in the sketch I drew. Five pairs of grey eyes cut into me, pleading with me to help them, and I didn't know how to.

"No!" I wailed. "No, don't hurt them, *please*."

"I have to hurt them." Morgan chuckled darkly. "I'm a Miles, and hurting the Slater brothers is what we do."

"No, please," I begged. "Don't hurt them … Hurt *me* instead."

"*You*?" he repeated, a quizzical look roaming over my body. "You want me to hurt *you*?"

Damien screamed around the cloth stuffed into his mouth as Morgan lowered to his hands and knees and approached me. His violet eyes never blinked, and once they locked on mine, they didn't stray. Tears flowed down my cheeks, and hiccups escaped my mouth, but my breathing stopped when Morgan climbed over me and pushed my legs apart.

"You don't really want Damien," Morgan said, then suddenly, he wasn't Morgan anymore; he was Dante Collins. "Ye' want me." His smile was so welcoming, and I wanted to feel relaxed in his presence … but I couldn't. "Ye' want me in your bed just like ye' had me there for four long months, workin' every knot out of your body with me cock and fingers. D'ye remember how loud I made you moan, Alannah? Ye' want *me* and *not* Damien because ye' can control how ye' feel about me. Ye' had me under your thumb, but ye' could never control how ye' felt about Damien. Isn't that right, beautiful?"

I closed my eyes, put my hands over my ears, and screamed. My hands were quickly pulled from my ears, and when I opened my eyes, Dante was gone, and Morgan was back. His smile was sinister, and I knew deep in my heart that he *was* going to hurt me.

"You can never get rid of me, angel," he said, moving his head closer to mine. "I'm inside your mind, and I'm *always* going to be there."

I whimpered.

"You're mine, angel," he almost growled like an animal making a claim. "You'll never be Damien's, not truly. You'll *always* be mine."

"Please," I pleaded. "Just let them go. If you're gonna hurt someone, hurt *me*. They've been through *enough*!"

Morgan blinked, and suddenly, a large blade appeared in his hand.

"Your request is a noble one, angel," he said. "And I'm going to grant it for you because you're precious to me."

I heard Damien's scream and the roars of his brothers when the sharp silver blade was placed on my throat and pressed roughly into my skin. It didn't sting or hurt in any way, but I felt the pressure of it when I swallowed.

"You'll *never* get rid of me."

With those words spoken, Morgan yanked his hand to the right, and when I tried to draw in a breath, I found I no longer could. I felt something wet run down my chest like a stream, and I could hear nail-biting, muffled screams fill my ears. I touched my hands to my chest and stomach, and when they came away stained with blood, my world went black. The last thing I saw was a grinning Morgan mouthing one word to me.

Mine.

CHAPTER TWO

I came awake with a start, and my hands instantly went to my neck. I felt nothing except the star pendant necklace that Damien had gifted to me six months prior. I touched my skin, feeling for a cut of some kind, and when I felt nothing, I sagged back into the mattress with relief. Realisation dawned on me that what happened wasn't real; it was just a nightmare. Morgan wasn't back, and Damien and his brothers were safe. I turned my head to my right and relaxed even more when I heard my love's soft snores. I couldn't see him because of how dark we needed our room to be able to fall asleep, but I could hear him, sense him, *feel* him.

When I shifted my body, he moved in his sleep and wrapped his arm around my waist, tugging me against his side. I loved that about him. No matter what, Damien had to have his hand on some part of my body as we slept. He had admitted to me that he sometimes woke up, and for a few moments, he felt like he dreamt of our coupling, but when he felt me under his palm, he knew I was his. In a way, I felt the same. It wasn't until I heard his snores after I awoke that I relaxed, knowing he was by my side.

Though after my nightmare, not even Damien's presence could comfort me.

I lifted my hand to my face and covered my mouth when tears welled in my eyes, and a soft cry escaped from my parted lips. I knew what happened was a nightmare and not real, but it had triggered a slow building panic attack. My heart pounded so fast against my chest that I could feel each thump as if it were a wallop. Fear wrapped around me as tight as Damien's arm, and I began to feel like the area around me was closing in. I roughly pushed Damien's arm away from my body, and the action caused him to wake instantly.

"What?" he said, groggily. "What's wrong?"

Without a word, I kicked away the blanket that covered me, got out of my bed, and blindly rushed over to the window. Pulling back the curtains, I unlocked the balcony door and opened it wide. The cool air that slammed into me felt like a smack in the face. I stepped out onto the balcony, but before I could touch my fingers to the rail, strong hands clamped down on my shoulders, and held me in place.

"Alannah!" Damien grunted as he roughly shook me. "Wake up."

"I'm already awake," I said, my breathing laboured. "But I can't breathe. I need air."

Damien stepped out onto the balcony with me, and when he looked down at me, he squinted his eyes as he used the street lamp light to see me. He frowned, lifted his hand, and used his thumb to swipe away the tears from my cheeks. I hadn't realised I was still crying.

"What's wrong, Alannah?"

I hesitated. "I had a nightmare."

There was no way I was going to tell him the content of my nightmare because Morgan Allen was *always* on Damien's mind, and I didn't want him to worry. If he knew I was having issues over him, he'd stress out more than he already was. I couldn't protect Damien from Morgan before, but I would do everything I could to protect him now.

Damien's frown deepened. "About what?"

I stepped forward and pressed my face against his hard chest, feeling soft chest hair brush against my skin. I wrapped my arms around his waist and sighed in contentment.

"I don't remember," I lied. "It was just a bad dream."

Damien's arms came around me. He rubbed his palms up and down my back and kissed the crown of my head.

"We're lucky we didn't have sex before bed," he commented lightly. "We'd be standing out here butt ass naked otherwise."

When I chuckled, Damien gave me a little squeeze.

"Are you okay?"

I nodded. "You're 'ere with me, so I'm fine."

We went back into our room, closing the balcony door behind us. Damien flipped on the light and then sat next to me on our bed. My hands were trembling, and he noticed. He kneeled before me and took my hands in his. I watched as he lifted them to his mouth and placed a gentle kiss on my knuckles. The gesture and being in his presence began to calm me, and it didn't take long for my shaking to stop. I had been having nightmares about Morgan on and off for a few weeks now, and each time, my thrashing woke Damien. He never complained, not once. He would just hold me until I relaxed. He seemed to know that he had to have his hands on me and be in my space for that to happen.

"Thank you."

Damien tilted his head to the side. "For what?"

"For sittin' with me while ye' calm me down."

He raised a brow.

"Ye' get this close to me and put your hands on me because it relaxes me," I said. "I've noticed it."

"Maybe I just wanna put my hands on you." He grinned. "Have you ever thought of that?"

When I smiled and a few tears fell from my eyes at the same time, Damien's smile disappeared. I hated that I had upset him, but tonight's nightmare really scared me. I couldn't talk to Damien about it without causing him more worry, and using my own mind to break it down had never worked out well for me in the past. In my dream, I was the one to die at the end, but Morgan usually killed

Damien while I screamed and pleaded for it to be me. I knew it was all fake, just my mind playing tricks on me, but the dreams always felt so real that I couldn't help but feel genuine fear.

"I'm okay," I said, still smiling as my tears fell. "I was due me period a few days ago, and that's what has me all teary."

I *was* due my period, but it wasn't what caused my tears. Damien leaned up and kissed my tear-stained cheeks. I closed my eyes, revelling in the sensation of his lips on my skin. I inhaled his scent, basked in his presence, and prayed to God that nothing would ever happen to this man because he was my heart.

"I love ye'," I said, my soul feeling like it was being crushed. "I love ye' so much, more than me life."

"Alannah." Damien frowned. "Baby, why are you so sad?"

Because I'm terrified of being without you.

"I don't know."

"Freckles, look at me." When I did, Damien leaned in and placed a gentle kiss on my lips. "I love you, too. Your nightmare has scared you, but it's not real. I'm right here with you. I'll always be here to protect you."

"Ye' don't know that," I whispered. "Ye' don't know that ye'll always be with me."

Damien stared at me. "Did something happen to *me* in your nightmare?" When I couldn't look him in the eye, he came to his own conclusions.

"Sweetheart"—he sighed—"please don't worry about what might or might not happen to me. You *know* what worrying about things you can't control does to your head."

It made me overthink and worry and stress.

"I know." I nodded, lifting a hand to wipe my cheeks. "I'm bein' stupid."

"You're *not* stupid," Damien stated softly. "You're just tired, and your nightmare is using your exhaustion to scare you."

I agreed with him.

"I'm sorry for wakin' ye'," I said as I glanced at the wall and saw it was only five to two. "Ye' must think I'm—"

"Beautiful when you're sleepy?" Damien cut me off. "You bet I do."

I smiled. "You're full of it."

I climbed back into our bed while Damien went to the bathroom. He turned off the light when he returned, cloaking the room in darkness. When the mattress dipped, and he lay back down, I rolled over to snuggle against his side straight away. I felt bad for waking him because I knew how tired he was. He had been working nonstop as of late, and he deserved a full night's rest even though he couldn't have that because of me. I kissed his chest just as his arm came around me.

"Do you want to have sex?"

I vibrated with silent laughter at his unexpected question.

"You're unbelievable."

Damien gave me a light squeeze. "I'm just checking to see if you want some of this before you go to sleep."

I heard in his voice how tired he was. If I said yes to having sex, he would fulfil my request, but I knew he didn't really want to do anything other than close his eyes and go to sleep.

"I'll have some of ye' in the mornin', big man," I answered with a forced yawn. "Go to sleep."

He didn't answer me, and I knew it was because he was already falling asleep. That was Damien's superpower. He was one of those sickening people who could fall asleep the second their head touched a pillow. I envied him for that, especially at the current moment when sleep was the last thing on my mind. I waited for ten long minutes, just to make sure he was in a deep sleep, before I slipped out of his hold. I tiptoed out of the bedroom and gently closed the door behind me.

I lifted the lid off the basket in the hallway that was full of clean, folded clothes. Taking off my pyjamas, I tossed them into the dirty wash basket in the bathroom and popped on my oversized white plaid shirt. As I buttoned it up and rolled the sleeves up to my elbows, my finger got snagged in a small hole. The shirt had seen better days; the wear and tear showed how old it was. It was a large shirt, long enough to cover my behind, so I didn't bother searching for leggings to put on. I checked on Barbara, who was asleep in the sitting room and clearly comfortable by the way she was positioned on the settee.

I cleaned out her litter tray and topped up her water before I ventured into my inner sanctum. Glancing around after I flipped on the light, the first thing I thought of was my dream, but I forced myself to push it to the back of my mind. I already had a mini breakdown over it, so I didn't need to give it any more thought. I couldn't help that Morgan entered my subconscious when I was asleep, but I'd be damned if he took over my mind while I was awake.

"He is gone," I told myself. "He has no power over you, Damien, or *anyone* else."

I inhaled and exhaled a deep breath before I got to work on a sketch of Ryder and Branna's twins, Nixon and Jules. Even though I worked on it whenever I had free time, it was coming together slower than I would have liked, and for some reason, I was sure it was because of my nightmares. Every nightmare I had seemed to drain me of life a small piece at a time, and I didn't know what to do about it. I wished I could talk to Damien about it, but he constantly thought of Morgan and played the what-if game when he thought back to our lives six months ago. And I found myself always assuring him that everything was okay when I needed that same reassurance.

I wanted to talk to Bronagh, but she already had her hands full with her family, and the fact she was nearly due her second baby. I didn't want to bother her or anyone else with my dumb, recurring issue. My parents were out of the question too; the three of us were preparing to get the results of my ma's recent mammogram to see if she was cancer free or if she had to go through more treatments. I had no one to confide in, meaning I only had myself to 'talk' to, and that led to me overthinking and making myself sick with worry.

Morgan had truly succeeded when he set out to get inside my

head. He didn't turn me away from the Slater brothers for good as he'd originally wanted, but he succeeded in making me doubt everything. Myself. Damien. My life. In my heart, I knew I was happy in my relationship, with my job, my friends, and my family ... but that was where the worry came in. I was terrified of losing everything I had. I knew what it felt like to be at rock bottom, and I feared feeling that emptiness again.

"Stop overthinkin'," I scowled at myself. "Just *stop*."

I shook my head and focused on my sketch. I immersed myself in my craft and got lost in the beauty of creating. I glanced at the clock on the wall to my right when I paused for a mini break. It was nearly four a.m., and that shocked me. Time had flown by as I worked. I rolled my neck onto my shoulders, grunting when I heard a satisfying *pop*.

"Freckles?"

I jerked my gaze over my shoulder, squinting my eyes in time to see Damien emerge from the shadows as he stepped into the room from the hallway. My eyes trailed down his form, and I swallowed. He was naked except for the black boxer briefs he wore, and gazing at his body caused a shiver to run the length of my spine. He was so deliciously beautiful that I wanted to run my tongue over every inch of him.

"Ye' scared me, Dame."

"Sorry," he said, his voice laced with sleep. "I woke up, and you weren't there."

I turned back to my easel.

"I couldn't sleep, so I thought I'd come in 'ere and do some sketchin'."

"When did you come in here?"

"After ye' fell back asleep earlier."

He sighed. "You should have woken me up."

"Why?" I questioned. "*You* could sleep, and *I* couldn't. It didn't make sense for me to stay in there and disrupt ye'."

He didn't answer. Instead, he came up behind me and rested his hands lightly on my hips, his thumbs playing with the fabric of my shirt. "What are you drawing, gorgeous?"

"See for yourself."

"Is that Jules … or Nixon?"

"It's Jules," I answered. "Nixon will go next to 'im."

"You're drawing the twins?"

I nodded as I used my finger to smooth out a harsh edge on Jules's earlobe.

"I want to surprise their parents with it. I haven't drawn the twins since they were newborns, and they're just over six months old now, so I wanted to fix that. I'm goin' to add Ry and Bran in the background, too."

"Babe, that's so sweet of you."

"Thanks. I think they'll love it."

I stiffened when Damien tugged my shirt up and slid his hands down from my hips to my behind, his fingers not so gently biting into my flesh.

"Don't even *think* about it," I playfully warned. "I'm busy."

"Please?" Damien murmured, nuzzling his face between my shoulder blades. "I woke up craving you, freckles."

I rolled my eyes but couldn't stop my lips from curving upwards at the corners.

"Ye' say that every single time ye' wake up with a stiffy."

Damien's chuckle was low. "That means I crave you."

"That's a cute way of sayin' ye' want to get your cock wet."

He didn't answer me; he was too busy sliding his hands down onto my bare mid-thighs. I turned to face him with a frown in place. Damien looked at my expression and smiled. He was tired—I could tell from how heavy his lids hung over his luminous grey eyes—but he still wanted me, and that caused me to pause.

"You have charcoal on your nose."

I wasn't surprised.

"Wipe it off."

"My hands are a little full at the minute."

He cupped my behind roughly, and when I scowled up at him, he grinned.

"Five minutes," he said. "I'll be quick."

"No, ye' won't," I countered. "Ye' say ye'll be quick, then when we get goin', ye'll take your feckin' time, and ye' *know* it."

Damien pressed his lips together, and when he smiled, his dimples creased his cheeks.

"If ye' get me into our bedroom, ye' *know* I'm gonna fall asleep by the time we're finished, and that means I'll be where I'm at right now with me sketch. Tonight is the first night in a long while that I've gotten a lot done on it."

"What if I don't *let* you sleep?"

I deadpanned. "Ye'll give in to me if I whine that I'm tired, and ye' know it."

Damien didn't disagree; he only dipped his head to hide his tantalising grin. He brushed the tip of his nose against mine and flexed his hands around my behind. The simple action sent a shiver racing up my spine, and my back involuntarily arched, pushing my breasts against Damien's chest. He hummed, seemingly satisfied, and before I could tell him to back off, his lips brushed over my jawline, then skimmed down my neck before they latched on my sweet spot where he sucked and flicked his tongue back and forth over the sensitive flesh.

"Damien."

The second I heard how breathless and needy my voice was when I moaned his name, I knew I was a goner.

"Bedroom," I rasped. "Now."

"No," he replied, feather kissing my neck. "I wanna fuck you in here."

My eyes crossed, too focused on the tingling sensation gifted by his lips.

"But—"

"No buts." Damien nipped my skin with his teeth. "Turn around and bend over."

14

My knees almost buckled beneath me, but when I swallowed and had control of myself, I turned around and shamelessly pushed my behind against Damien's erect cock, making him hiss. A smirk curved at my lips, but it was wiped away when I was bent forward over my desk, and Damien's hand came down and swatted my behind. I yelped in surprise.

"Damien!"

He chuckled, darkly. "That'll teach you to tease me."

"I can't believe ye' just—*Damien*!"

The invasion of his warm, wet tongue against my underwear had me balling my hands into fists. I groaned out loud when my knickers were tugged to the side, and Damien licked up and down my slit before he plunged his tongue deep inside me. I bucked my hips back against his face, and he chuckled.

"You *always* try to fuck my mouth when I have you positioned like this."

"Because," I hissed, "it feels fuckin' amazin'."

His hands moved up to my behind, and he squeezed me.

"Let me hear you," Damien said before he resumed his toe-curling torture.

I couldn't contain my moans if someone had paid me to do so. I was sure I could give a porn star a run for her money, and when I once told Damien that, he wholeheartedly agreed. I was not a silent lover, and Damien loved *that*.

"Damien," I rasped. "Please, no more. Just fuck me already."

Usually, I loved when he tongued me to orgasm, but at times, I just needed to have him fuck me into bliss. This was one of those times. I licked my lips when his mouth moved upwards. He kissed my arse, then my lower back, pushing my shirt upwards as he moved. Then he fisted his hand in my hair and tugged on it until my back was arched.

"I love fucking you when your spine is curved like this," Damien hummed as he flattened his palm on my lower back. "Keep that arch."

When he suddenly thrust into me, I lost the arch for about a second before Damien tugged on my hair once more until I got it back.

"I'm gonna kill you for pullin' me ... fuck! Do it *harder*!"

Damien's chuckle was low as he fucked me and pulled my hair at the same time. I never like my hair being touched until he set a steady pace and my body confused the stinging pain with pleasure. It wasn't much, but it gave me a thrill each time he pulled on it and slammed into me at the same time.

"Do you know how fucking sexy it is to watch my cock slide in and out of you?" Damien grunted as the sound of skin slapping against skin filled the silent room. "I want to bite your ass when your flesh jiggles as I slam into you. Christ, you really are ... so. Fucking. Sexy."

I pushed back against him, earning a hiss and another swat to my behind.

"So demanding," Damien mused.

I reached down to my parted thighs and played with my clit as he fucked me, and when I brought myself to the edge of an orgasm, my body became tense.

"I love you," he rasped. "You're about to come. I can feel you tighten around ... Fu ... *uck*."

I drew in a sharp breath as my orgasm slammed into me and spread out over my body like molten lava. The heated bliss wrapped around my muscles and soothed them until they were soft like jelly. I heard my cries, my screams and pleas for Damien to fuck me harder, to prolong the sensation of delight that filled me. I could feel bites of pain mixed in with my pleasure, and it only heightened the experience. When the pulses slowed, and the pleasure slowly faded, only relaxation and exhaustion remained.

"Good girl." Damien panted as he withdrew from me and placed a kiss on each arse cheek. "Fuck, that felt awesome."

"Why am I a good girl?" I asked, my eyes closed as I continued to lay spread out over my desk. "What'd I do?"

"You tightened your pussy muscles when I asked you to," Damien replied. "It made me come harder."

I hummed. "I didn't even hear ye' ask me that."

"You didn't?"

I shook my head.

"Are you ... Don't you *dare* fall asleep on your desk!"

I groaned as he pulled me upright, and he laughed when I turned and sagged against him.

"I told ye' I'd be tired and sleepy. I *told* ye' so."

I didn't even make a sound when Damien lifted me into his arms and carried me into our bathroom where I tiredly cleaned myself up. A little light from the approaching sunrise peeked in through a slit in our bedroom curtains, but neither of us got up to fix them once we got into bed. I snuggled against Damien, and once I threw my leg over his body and my arm over his stomach, anything but sleeping became impossible.

"I love you, freckles."

I was already falling asleep, and Damien's soft laughter was the last thing I heard.

CHAPTER THREE

We both managed to sleep for a few hours until our responsibilities forced us to get up—Barbara and Damien's job. We were both lounging about in our sitting room on our settee, snuggled next to each other. Both of us were on our phones. I was working, and Damien was scrolling through Facebook.

"I think I've found a new assistant."

The words had barely left my mouth before Damien snatched my phone from my hands to study the profile of the woman I was considering to hire to run my website and handle my hectic email and calendar online. I didn't get mad; I simply folded my arms across my chest and waited. He needed to read up on this new person who would possibly be entering my life so he knew every detail about her to relax himself. It was the least I could do, considering how against he was about me finding a new assistant in the first place.

"It's an *online job* this time," Damien said, looking from the phone to me, "right?"

My lips twitched.

"Right." I nodded. "I'm confident she isn't a ghost from your shady past comin' back to haunt ye' by gettin' inside me head and turnin' me against your family. I think that only happens once in a lifetime, love."

Damien scowled at my teasing, not in the slightest bit impressed, and returned his attention to the device in his hand.

"It happened before, so it could happen again."

I wanted to say with confidence that he was wrong, but I couldn't. The truth was that Morgan Allen, who was really Carter Miles—a once childhood friend of Damien hell-bent on revenge—made it an easy task to turn me against the Slater brothers in order to hurt them for the murder of his brother and uncle. Morgan had entered my life and my home with a shocking amount of ease. I knew Damien was scared that another person with ulterior motives could possibly do the same, but I believed I wasn't as naïve as I once was. The things I now knew about Damien and his family, the things I had learned about while being too trusting with Morgan, were always front and centre in my mind. I learned a lot from that experience, and while it emotionally ruined me for a while, I wouldn't change it for the world.

It helped me grow as a person, even if I was struggling as of late with nightmares because of it.

"Morgan *isn't* comin' back," I said, repeating the same thing I had told Damien a million times in the six months since Morgan left our lives after he turned it upside down. "Ye' heard 'im. He just wanted to manipulate me and turn me against ye' because he knew it would hurt you and your brothers."

"He succeeded for a time, Alannah," Damien said, his jaw tight. "I just thank God you saw through his bullshit and saw my truth."

I thanked God for that, too.

"Would ye' feel better if it was someone we *know* who helped me?"

That got my better half's full attention.

"Who do you have in mind?"

"Bronagh," I answered with a shrug. "She's surprisingly handy on a computer; she's been helpin' me since everythin' with Morgan went to shite. The only thing I can credit 'im with is how organised he made everythin'. Me and Bee have just been followin' the system he set up, and it's workin' a charm. I've never had so many clients book me in advance. I mean, ye've seen me calendar. I'm booked for the next seven months with projects. The only time I can make room for someone is when I have a cancelation."

The second I finished speaking, Damien leaned over and surprised me by covering my mouth with his. When he pulled back, I blinked.

"Not that I don't love you kissin' me whenever ye' want, but what was *that* for?"

"For suggesting Bee help you instead of a stranger," he answered, and I could see the relief in his grey eyes. "Please hire her. It will make me feel immensely better if Bronagh helps you and not a newcomer."

He just made my decision for me.

"Then I'll ask 'er," I said, snuggling into his side. "Ye' need to relax about this, though, Dame. It's not healthy to be lookin' over your shoulder every two seconds, thinkin' someone is gonna snatch me away from ye'."

I felt like a hypocrite for telling him to relax when I worried about the same thing. Only not me being taken from him, but him being taken from me.

"I can't help fearing that." He sighed. "Jesus, Lana, I can't imagine my life without you. I'd be broken … good for absolutely nothing if I lost you."

I moved, cocked my leg over his body, and straddled him, placing my hands on either side of his face.

"I'm 'ere with *you*, Dame," I said, leaning in and resting my forehead against his. "I'm not goin' anywhere, sweetheart."

Damien closed his eyes and inhaled deeply. I looked into his eyes when he opened them, and I smiled. His breath caught a little.

"You're beautiful."

I ducked my head, making him chuckle.

"Alannah?"

"Hmm?"

"Will you marry me?"

I leaned back and looked down at him as I said, "No."

Damien looked away from me; a deep hurt that he couldn't hide played out on his face like the two other times he asked me to marry him in the past six months. And just like those two other times, saying no left a bitter taste in my mouth.

"Damien," I said, brushing my nose against his cheek. "You *know* how I feel about things movin' too fast with us. I don't want to jinx what we have."

"Is what we have solid?" he asked, and when I nodded, he said, "Then *why* won't you say yes when I ask you to marry me?"

"Because we're together *six months*," I stressed. "When we do things too fast, bad things happen, and I don't want to ruin our relationship."

"I want to marry you," Damien pressed. "That's not going to change. You *said* you wanted to marry me and have loads of babies. I want that *now*."

I knew he wanted that. Especially now that Kane and Aideen had recently tied the knot in the city's registry office and became husband and wife, quickly followed by Alec and Keela a week later who didn't want a traditional church wedding. Ever since both couples got married, Damien had been adamant about us moving to the next stage of our relationship. He saw three of his brothers blissfully married with gorgeous kids, and his twin happily engaged with a beautiful child and expecting one more, and he wanted that *badly*.

"I *do* want to marry ye' and have babies, but not right—"

"I'm going to be late for work." He cut me off, the muscles in his jaw rolling back and forth. "I'd better get going."

I didn't move.

"Ye' can't just leave when we're talkin' about this, Damien," I argued. "Nothin' good comes from lettin' a conversation like this lie. Ye' *know* that."

"We've said what needs to be said," he countered. "I want to marry you, and you don't want to marry me. I get it. Now, get off me because I have to go to work."

Like the flip of a switch, my mood turned sour.

"You're an arsehole," I grouched as I scrambled off him and stormed out of the room, heading towards the bedroom. "Ye' can't resist startin' a fight when ye' don't get what ye' want."

"I'm not bitching about not getting my way, Alannah," Damien shouted from behind me. "I'm pissed off because you won't take the next step with me."

"Because I'm not ready yet!" I bellowed, turning in the bedroom doorway in time to see Damien reach for the handle of the front door. "Why can't ye' just *wait* a while?"

"Because I love you and want to spend the rest of my life with you."

"And you need to put a weddin' band on me finger right this second to assure yourself that's gonna happen?" I shook my head. "I *will* marry ye'. I'm *goin'* to marry ye', but when *I'm* ready, Damien."

"Yeah," he snapped back. "I got that, loud and fucking clear. Everything will be on *your* time. Your way or the highway, right?"

"Fuck you!"

"Later." His lip curled upward into a sneer. "I have work to get to, but I'll keep thinking of your sweet pussy to make my day go by faster."

I loathed when he was like this. He could rival Nico Slater, his twin brother, with how much of an arsehole he could become when he was upset about something. With a fierce scowl sent in his direction, I slammed the bedroom door shut. A second later, the apartment front door rapped against the wood of the door panel, causing a loud bang to echo.

"Arsehole!" I bellowed, loud enough for Damien to hear me in the hallway. "If ye' break that door, you're fuckin' payin' for it!"

I could have sworn I heard his humourless laughter.

"Bloody man," I scowled and angrily folded my arms across my chest as I tapped my foot against the floor. "He makes me so *mad*, Barbara!"

Barbara, my eleven-month-old cat, jumped up onto my bed and rubbed her head against my hip. I turned my attention to her and relaxed as I petted her. I climbed up onto my bed and flopped onto my back. When she crawled up onto my stomach, I chuckled as she sat down and claimed my belly as her throne. I found her when she was roughly ten weeks old, and the few weeks that followed my finding her were the best and worst weeks of my life. From entering my relationship with Damien to learning my mother had breast cancer … as well as secrets about my best friends that shook my entire world to its core. Not to mention Morgan Allen's entry into my life, the bearer of those haunting secrets I had learned about the Slater brothers.

"Stupid girl," I scowled to myself.

Thinking of how trusting I was with someone who could have been potentially dangerous towards me left me nothing but irritated. I was a smart woman, but I had made some shitty decisions in my past. Morgan was one of them, which was worth an eye roll because I had once thought he was a blessing who came to me just when I needed him.

I knew his name was Carter Miles, but in my head, he was Morgan Allen.

For weeks, I worked in my home office with him, organising and running my business. While building what I thought was a friendship with him, I was shocked to find out his goal, and overall purpose in my life, was to turn me against the Slater brothers. He succeeded for a couple of weeks, but when I did the smart thing and heard Damien and everyone else out, I learned why they had to commit such acts of horror.

They were left with no choice.

I grabbed my phone from my nightstand when it rang and answered it without looking at who was calling.

"Hello?"

"I want to die."

I grinned. "What's the matter?"

"This baby needs to be born right *now*," Bronagh stated. "I can't handle bein' pregnant for much longer. I feel like a balloon that's about to pop."

"Imagine how Keela feels. 'Er due date is *today,* and there is no sign of 'er havin' the baby."

"I know," Bronagh groaned. "But she can go at any time. I still have a week and a bit left."

"Have sex," I encouraged. "Wild, rough sex. That should get things movin'."

"We can't 'cause it hurts me too much when Dominic gets into a rhythm," Bronagh explained. "We haven't had sex in over three weeks, and he's gonna have to suffer until six weeks *after* I have the baby … He'll probably leave me for some woman with a perfectly functionin' fanny."

When I laughed, it irritated Barbara. She jumped off the bed and walked over to the window where she jumped up on the windowsill without a backward glance.

"It's not funny!"

I continued to laugh.

"I'm sorry," I stressed. "I'm takin' this seriously, I swear."

"Great, 'ere come the waterworks." Bronagh sniffled. "I'm sick of cryin' over nothin'."

"I know, babe, but ye' *will* have the baby soon, and then ye'll be cryin' for a different reason. Like gettin' no sleep."

Bronagh snickered a little. "What're ye' doin'?"

"Lyin' in bed … thinkin' of how to murder Damien and get away with it."

Silence.

"What'd he do?"

"He asked me to marry 'im, again, and when I said no, he became alpha arsehole."

"Did you explain why—"

"Of course," I cut Bronagh off. "I told 'im that I'm not ready yet. I love 'im to death, Bronagh, and I *will* marry 'im, but is it so terrible that I want things to just progress a little slower?"

"No, it's not terrible. What's terrible is Damien throwin' a wobbler 'cause he isn't gettin' his way."

"That exactly what I said to 'im!"

"How'd he take it?"

"He had an attitude, then left for work." I huffed. "He's put me in a foul mood."

"He'll come home grovellin' for your forgiveness." Bronagh snorted. "That man is so in love with ye' he can't stand when you're mad at 'im."

"I wish he wasn't as grouchy."

"Babe, you've got the calm twin. Imagine how *I* feel."

"*Please.*" I snorted. "It's Nico I feel sorry for when ye' both argue. You're a nightmare."

"Hey," Bronagh jokingly quipped. "I'm a lot more mellow than I used to be."

"Since you had Georgie," I agreed. "But ye' can also be a total mama bear, so I'm not sure if mellow is the right word."

"Bitch."

I chuckled. "Do ye' want to go to the village for somethin' to eat? I'd murder a breakfast roll."

"Oh, *hell* yeah. I want two of them."

Commenting on how bad two full-size breakfast rolls would be on her body would most likely result in my death, so I kept my mouth shut.

"I'll swing by and get ye' in ten minutes."

"Deal. Me and Georgie will be ready. Beep when you're outside."

After I hung up with Bronagh, I got changed into a knee-length sky blue dress with black sandals and tied my hair up into a high ponytail. It was early June, and things were hotter than usual for this time of the year ... or for Ireland, in general. It was only ten a.m., and it was twenty-six degrees outside with no clouds in sight. It was roasting, and summer had only *just* started. It was like all my Christmases came at once. After I made sure that Barbara had food, water, and free run of my apartment, I left with my side bag and keys in hand. When I exited the elevator in the lobby, I groaned out loud when I saw two men walking towards me.

"Well, well, well … aren't you lookin' good enough to eat."

I raised a brow at Dante Collins and rolled my eyes.

"Damien will lynch ye' if he hears ye' sayin' stuff like that to me."

"He can try."

Dante's grin told me that he was only teasing, but I still had to warn him to knock it off. The last thing I needed was for Damien and him to fight again. The last time resulted in bruises and sore egos, and I did not want to deal with either. Assuring Damien that my four-month fling with Dante was nothing for him to worry about took time, and Dante knew that, which was why he got a kick out of tormenting me. As I stared at Dante, I thought back to when I had a discussion with him on the phone a few months ago about how that day panned out.

"I want to apologise."

"For what?"

"For how I spoke about you in the garage back when you and Damien got together a few weeks ago... and I'm also sorry for smackin' your arse."

I grunted as I adjusted my phone against my ears. "Continue."

"I'm sick with meself for talkin' about ye' like ye' were an object and treatin' ye' the way I did, and in front of the lads, too."

"Why are ye' bringin' this up now?" I asked. "It's been ages since that happened."

"I know, but I never apologised for it."

"I won't lie. It did hurt me feelin's."

"I know ... I just ... me own feelin's were hurt."

I blinked. "Yours?"

"Yeah," Dante continued. "I guess I was a little ... jealous."

"Jealous?"

"Of Damien."

"Why?" I asked, shocked. "Why would you be jealous of 'im?"

"Because he had you."

My heart stopped. "Date."

"Don't freak out. I'm not in love with ye' ... I just could have been, ye' know? I really liked ye'."

This was entirely new information.

I sat down. "I never intended to lead ye' on. I swear."

"Babe, I know that. Ye' were upfront with me. I just caught a few feelin's, and that's not your fault. Don't worry, though, we're square now. You're happy, and I'm happy for ye'."

"We have to get ye' a girlfriend, so ye' can be just as happy as me."

"Leave me be, woman." Dante laughed. "I have many women to tumble with under me bed sheets before I settle down. Not every woman can tame me like you can."

"Ye'd be surprised." I snorted. "It's the quiet ones ye' have to watch out for."

I came back to the present and grinned at Dante.

"When ye' get a girlfriend, I'm gonna tell 'er all the things ye' did to me just to piss ye' off when ye' have to calm 'er down when she gets jealous."

"Piss me off or turn me on?"

I swiped at him, but he jumped out of my reach, chuckling.

"I'm only jokin', me and Damien are square ... he knows we're only mates."

Damien *hated* that I was friends with Dante, and I understood why, so to avoid awkward run-ins, I rarely came by Damien's job at the garage. I doubted Damien would ever fully relax around Dante until he had a girlfriend himself. Meetings like this couldn't be avoided now that Dante lived in the same building as me and Damien. Along with Harley, JJ, Gavin, and his pregnant non-girlfriend,

Kalin. Kane, being the landlord, hooked up Aideen's brothers and was the reason they were my new neighbours.

"Did ye' put sunscreen on?" Harley asked me, reminding me of his presence. "It's hot as a motherfucker out there."

"I put some on, and I've a bottle in me bag for top ups. Thanks, Da."

Dante snickered, and Harley grinned.

"Smartarse."

My lips twitched. "Why're ye' both 'ere? Shouldn't ye' be in work?"

"We popped out for a minute," Dante answered.

"And you came home instead of enjoyin' that fine weather outside?"

"We're checkin' on Gavin," Harley explained. "He called in sick to work, but Ryder could have sworn he heard a woman moan in pleasure in the background. Date thinks he was watchin' porn, but *I* think little brother is mattress dancin' with Kalin, and since *we* have to pick up his slack for not bein' at work for the early shift, I wanna know how *sick* he is. I'm gonna deck 'im if he's anythin' less than half dead with the flu."

Gavin was in a bit of a pickle, to say the least.

I didn't know the entire story, not *yet* anyway, but Gavin had gotten a woman pregnant, a woman who he had been having sex with on and off for months. Her name was Kalin Harris, and after some sort of family issues, she had nowhere to stay. Super landlord Kane came to the rescue and situated her in an apartment of her own … directly across the hall from Gavin's apartment. She was currently seven and half months pregnant with the next Collins baby. I found out about her existence and her pregnancy when she was only six weeks into it. A lot had changed since then, and apparently so had her relationship with Gavin, if moans of pleasure were put on the table.

Gavin had sworn to me that things were platonic between he and Kalin, and that they were going to co-parent and raise their son together as best as they could. Aideen had taken Kalin under her wing since we all found out about her. We had all attended a gender reveal party, a baby shower, and many girls' nights in to get to know one another. Kalin was kind of a part of our group at this point ... but I couldn't stand her. I backed her and Gavin one hundred percent in raising their son, but Kalin rubbed me the wrong way. She gave me, and only me, dirty looks whenever I was in her presence, and God forbid if I hugged Gavin or smiled at him when she was in viewing distance.

She didn't like me, and that pissed me off because I had been nothing but nice to her and tried to make her feel welcome from the second I had met her. It didn't help that I threw water in her face at her gender reveal party two weeks ago when she asked me to leave because I was the first person to hug Gavin when the blue balloons came out of the reveal box. I didn't *mean* to hug him first, or steal her thunder, but I was right next to him, and *he* looked at *me* first when it was revealed he was going to have a son. We're best friends, and we hugged because that was what we did ... but Kalin hated it.

I hadn't spoken to her or Gavin in the two weeks since. Of course, he sided with Kalin and so did nearly everyone else because, at the end of the day, all they saw was me throwing a water in a heavily pregnant woman's face and ruining her gender reveal party. It was a shitty situation, one that I still couldn't believe had taken place, but it was what it was, and I just had to roll with the punches and deal with the aftermath.

"If Kalin has Gavin in 'er apartment, she won't give 'im back. She has claws, *big* claws."

"She's shorter than *you*, and a might nicer, which is sayin' somethin' because you're just about the sweetest woman I know."

I rolled my eyes at Dante's description.

"She is a bitch who just happens to be short, Date. That's it."

"Who threw water in whose face at the gender reveal party of my nephew?"

I scowled at Dante. "I'm not proud of that."

"I *still* can't believe ye' did it." He snickered. "I haven't laughed that hard in a long time."

I could remember his laughing and his da advancing on him with a glare to silence him.

"It was a shitty situation, that's all."

Harley sighed. "The pair of ye' need to work things out, Lana."

I once hated that nickname because it reminded me of Damien, who was the one to give it to me, but everyone called me it now. Freckles was the only nickname that was reserved for Damien alone.

"Why should I work things out with 'er, Harls?"

"Because Gavin is losin' his mind tryin' to be the buffer between ye' both."

"She hates me 'cause I'm Gavin's best friend. She clearly has insecurities to work through if she thinks I'm a threat. Bronagh is his best mate too, but she doesn't glare or act up with *her*. Everyone knows I'm with Damien, and that I love 'im. Gavin has always been me best friend, and if she doesn't believe us when we tell 'er that, then that's *her* issue, *not* mine."

Harley sighed. "Alannah—"

I walked around the brothers and headed towards the lobby exit.

"I'm *done* talkin' about Kalin Harris," I cut him off. "Go check on Gavin. The poor bastard is probably balls deep inside the miniature Satan."

I could hear both of their sighs, but luckily, they didn't come after me. I exited my building and groaned in delight when licks of the hot sun covered my exposed skin. I forced all thoughts of the Collins brothers and Kalin to the back of my mind as I approached my car. I sang along to the radio on my journey to Bronagh and Nico's house. I beeped when I was outside, but I still got out of the car to help Bronagh with my niece and her things when they exited their house.

"Georgie," I beamed, hunkering down and opening my arms wide as she wobbly walked towards me. "You're gettin' *so* big, baby."

She was growing up before my eyes. She was fifteen months old now, Locke was nearly ten months, and Jax was *eighteen* months ... almost bloody two! It felt like just yesterday we were celebrating his first birthday. Before we knew it, he would be eighteen and causing men everywhere to have chest pains at the thought of him dating their daughters.

"Yana!" She squealed when I lifted her into the air.

Yana was as close to Lana as she could say, but she could say it the clearest out of everyone in our group so that made me happy. I tugged on her dark brown mini pigtails, and it made her giggle. She had matching dimples when she smiled, and that was the only thing of her father that I could see in her.

"Ye' birthed a clone of yourself," I said to Bronagh as she waddled towards me with a baby bag strapped over her shoulder. "Ye' realise that, right?

"Yup," she beamed. "The rest of the tribe can look like Dominic; I'm just glad I got one who looks like me."

"Are you bringin' a buggy?"

"Nah," she answered. "We're only goin' from the car to the café and back. Georgie will be fine walkin' with us. It'll be more practice for 'er."

I roamed my eyes over my friend and swallowed. She was huge, and I hated saying that because I knew it meant she was likely going to have a big chunky baby if she wasn't carrying much fluid. Her belly had dropped considerably since I last saw her two days ago which meant the baby was due to make an appearance at any moment. She literally looked like she was going to give birth at any second, which was crazy, because Keela looked like she could easily be five months pregnant instead of full term.

"Don't look at me like that."

I blinked. "Like what?"

"Like you're scared to go anywhere with me."

"But Bee—"

"No buts," she cut me off. "We're goin' for breakfast, or I'm gonna eat *you*."

I looked at Georgie. "Should we listen to 'er?"

The little cutie smiled and nodded like she understood what I was saying, which made me laugh.

"Okay, let me get 'er into the car seat, then I'll help ye'."

Bronagh didn't argue as I got Georgie into the baby seat I bought ages ago for my car. Once she was strapped in and secured, I moved to help Bronagh. She looked so swollen, but I didn't want to comment on it. I helped her into the passenger side, then jogged around to the driver's side and buckled myself in.

"Does Nico know you're leavin' the house?"

Bronagh didn't look at me, so I groaned as I took out my phone and dialled his number.

"What's up, little sis?"

I grinned. "Your child bearer and offspring are in me car."

Bronagh snorted.

"*Why* are they in your car?"

"Because we're goin' to get breakfast, but Bronagh hasn't told ye', so *I* have to so ye' don't blow a fuse when ye' find out."

Nico grunted. "Put her on the phone."

Bronagh heard him and shook her head.

"She said no."

"She'll be the death of me," he grumbled. "Lana, you *see* how pregnant she is, right?"

"Yeah … but she also threatened to eat *me* if I don't bring 'er for breakfast, so she's kind of winnin' 'ere, Nico."

"Alannah."

"She's hangry."

He paused. "What?"

"Hangry is when a person becomes an entitled arsehole because they neglected to feed themselves."

"Bronagh," Nico answered instantly. "What you just described is Bronagh."

"I know, so that's why I need to feed 'er."

He sighed. "Where are you guys going?"

"The village," I answered. "Hardly any walkin' is involved for 'er. I'll have 'er and the princess back home before ye' know it."

"You'll text me when you get them home?"

"I promise."

He caved. "Take care of my girls, Alannah."

"With me life, bro."

I could hear the smile in his voice when he said, "Bye."

It took fifteen minutes for us to reach the village, and when we parked and walked towards the café, we were delighted to find it was virtually empty, which meant we got to pick any table we wanted to sit at. Georgie babbled away to herself as I got her strapped into a high chair while Bronagh's eyes flew over the menu like it was her last supper.

"I know you're big and close to havin' this baby, but ye' definitely haven't put on half of the weight ye' did when ye' were pregnant with Georgie."

Bronagh beamed. "I know. I've been eatin' real good this time around and exercisin' with Dominic a few times a week. This week, I'm indulgin' because I'm close to the end so I don't mind."

"Your tits are *huge*," I added in a whisper. "Like, seriously. Huge."

Bronagh looked down at her chest.

"Me milk has come back in," she explained. "After Georgie stopped breastfeedin', they went back to their normal size, but now they're like mangos all over again. Dominic loves them."

"I feckin' bet he does."

Bronagh snickered. "Tell me about Damien."

"Nothin' to tell." I shrugged. "He wants to get married right now, and I wanna wait a while."

"How long do you wanna wait?"

"I don't know. I just don't wanna rush it, that's all."

"I'm sure Damien knows that. He is just … impatient."

"I know he loves me, Bronagh." I frowned. "I love 'im too. I just wanna relax a little."

"You're not askin' for much, Lana."

"Damien thinks I am."

"He'll realise how demandin' he is bein'. Just wait and see."

At the thought of Damien, I remembered our agreement over my assistant job.

"I have somethin' to ask ye'," I said to Bronagh. "If ye' want to say no, then say it. Don't just agree just because you're me friend."

Bronagh blinked. "You're not gonna ask me to do somethin' illegal, are ye'?"

I giggled. "No."

"Oh, fire away then."

"Before we argued this mornin', I was talkin' to Damien about me assistant job … and … and I wanted to offer it to *you*."

"Me?"

Her eyes were as wide as saucers.

"Yeah." I chuckled. "You."

"Ye' want *me* to be your assistant?"

"Why not?" I quizzed. "Ye've been doin' the job the past few months anyway."

"Yeah, but that was just helpin'. I told ye' I don't mind helpin' ye'."

"I mind," I said. "You're doin' a job, so I want to pay ye' for it. There is no one I trust more to fill this position, and Damien agrees with me."

"I don't know what to say."

"Ye' can talk to Nico about it before ye' decide."

"No way," Bronagh beamed. "I'll take the job. He will be delighted. I can do your emails, calendar, and other stuff when Georgie is nappin'. Even with a new baby, it'll be easy 'cause I do so much of it on me phone. When I need to use a desktop, I can just come around to yours."

"So you're me assistant?"

"I'm your assistant!"

I laughed. "Ye' don't even know how much you're gonna be paid."

"It'll be more than enough, knowin' you. I can't believe we're gonna work together."

Together, we chatted about Bronagh's new job, then the new baby, and everyone else in our lives. I wished I could slip my nightmares into the conversation, but I didn't want to worry her. An hour and a half and four phone calls from Nico later, I was leaving the café with Georgie on my hip and Bronagh waddling behind me. I sensed when she stopped walking, and when I turned to see what she was doing, I groaned out loud.

"Don't do it," I said as my best friend stared at the chocolate goodness displayed in the bakery window. "If Harry Potter can go from bein' a lonely boy livin' in a cupboard under the stairs to defeatin' the most evil wizard of all time *while* pullin' his best mate's sister in the process, then *you* can walk past this bakery with your head held high."

"Harry had a magical wand, though." Bronagh groaned. "I don't even have willpower."

"This day is gonna be a bust." I facepalmed myself with my free hand while Georgie rested her head on my shoulder. "We're *past* overindulgin' at this point."

"Can we get a cream bun then if it's already a bust?" my friend asked, licking her lips. "I've been good me entire pregnancy ... Today can just be a really *long* cheat day."

It was embarrassing how little convincing I needed.

"Fine ... but get me two of the cream buns and a slice of that chocolate truffle cake in the window ... oh, and a cup of hot chocolate with extra marshmallows. Fuck it, I'll just come in with ye'."

Bronagh rubbed her hands together. "Mama is eatin' *good* today."

When we left the bakery, I had a bag full of calories and could already feel the guilt that eating them would cause. By the time I got back to Bronagh's house, I was on my second slice of truffle cake, and guilt was suddenly the *last* thing on my mind.

"If I gain back the weight I lost six months ago, I'm gonna kill ye'."

Bronagh snorted as she finished her hot chocolate from the reusable flask she purchased.

"I'm not forcin' ye' to eat anythin'."

"Ye' aren't stoppin' me either."

When she made a move towards me, I hissed, "Try to take this cake away from me. I feckin' *dare* ye'."

When she cackled, I had to fight off a smile. I glanced at Georgie, who was playing in the corner with her toys, then focused on finishing my slice of heaven. I left a large bite for Georgie, who came over to me when I called her. She ate the cake, got it all over her mouth and had a massive grin on her face while doing so. I took a selfie of us and posted it as my new Facebook profile picture. I looked at my phone when it rang, and when I saw it was Nico, I answered it and said, "Tallaght morgue, you kill them, we chill them. How can I help ye'?"

"There is so much wrong with you that it's not even funny."

"What do ye' want, loser?" I grinned. "You're stalkin' me phone all mornin'."

"Where are you guys?"

"At the hospital," I answered. "Bronagh has given birth to twin girls. Congratulations, *Daddy*."

"I hate you."

"Relax the cacks." I snickered. "She's still up the duff with *one* baby."

"You aren't good for my heart. I hope you realise that."

I was thoroughly amused.

"Bronagh and Georgie are fine, alpha daddy. We're all at your house doin' absolutely nothin'."

"Good. Tell Bronagh a pipe burst in the ladies' showers, so the place is closing while it's being fixed. That means I'll be home in ten minutes."

"Yay," I said dryly. "Ye'll be 'ere to annoy us in person instead of callin' us every five minutes. Fantastic."

He hung up on me, and it made me laugh as I turned to Bronagh.

"A pipe burst so he gets to come home. He'll be 'ere in ten minutes."

"Did he hang up on ye'?"

"Yup."

She snorted. "He thinks ye' torment 'im more since you and Damien got together."

"He does?"

"Yup." Bronagh grinned. "He thinks ye' act like a bratty little sister."

"Then I must play me role accordingly and annoy 'im whenever possible."

When the three of us moved into the sitting room, I phoned Keela to see how she was doing.

"What's the crack?" she answered on the third ring.

"What's good, preggers?" I smiled as Georgie settled next to me on the settee. "Are ye' still pregnant?"

"Yup." She laughed. "But I may give birth out of absolute rage."

"Uh-oh, what's goin' on?"

"Alec has gone to get the messages in Aldi, and he said I wasn't allow to do any cleanin', but the windows are *filthy*."

"I absolutely hate agreein' with Alec, ye' know I do ... but ye' can't clean the windows. That involves stretchin' ... and a ladder."

Keela groaned, long and hard, and it made me grin.

"I've got ye', preggers," I said with certainty. "Auntie Alannah is on the case."

CHAPTER FOUR

I f Keela ever said I didn't do anything for her, I was going to kick her up the arse.

"Is the smudge gone?" I hollered. "Say yes, 'cause me arm is goin' dead buffin' this stupid thing."

For the past forty minutes, I had been Keela's cleaning mule, following her every order. I had cleaned six windows, inside and outside, and was on the seventh and final one for the front of the house. It just happened to be her and Alec's bedroom window, and it was the dirtiest pane of glass I had ever encountered because it took a hell of a scrub and buff to make it come up gleaming.

"Ye' put your hand on the glass, and I can see your handprint from all the way down 'ere."

I closed my eyes and began to count to ten.

"Which side is the handprint on?" I shouted and opened my eyes, roaming them over the window. "I can't see anythin'."

"It's to your right—"

"What the fuck are you *doing*, Alannah Ryan?"

Oh, Alec just full named me.

"I'm gettin' ready to take flight … What does it *look* like I'm doin', dumbarse?"

"It looks like you're standing on a slanted ladder, Alannah," he replied. "I go grocery shopping and come back to find you suicidal."

I lifted a hand and blindly waved away Alec's concern.

"It's grand. *I'm* grand."

"You're going to fall."

"Am not," I shouted. "Keela, which side is the handprint on?"

"Your lower right-hand side."

"Alannah, ignore my pregnant demon and listen to *me*," Alec snapped. "Get. The. Hell. Down!"

"Don't give me an order, Alec Slater!" I hollered back. "I can clean the outside of this bleedin' window with no problem. I'm helpin' Keela since she can't do this 'erself. I'm a good bloody friend who can do this. I don't need ye' hasslin' me so feck off."

"Shut it down before you hurt yourself, Jackie Chan."

I ignored Alec and continued to buff the window with my trusty newspaper.

"We get it, Lana," Ryder's voice shouted from across the road. "You're an independent woman who doesn't need a man, but seriously, don't go any higher. You're scared of heights, kid."

I paused. If Ryder was home, that most likely meant Damien was home because they took their breaks together.

"Alannah, get your ass *down*."

And there he was.

"Don't tell me what to do either, dickhead."

"Oh," Keela squealed. "I *love* when she curses; it sounds so strange comin' from 'er."

"Try living with her," Damien said, his voice louder than it needed to be. "She can give Bronagh a run for her money."

Lies. No one could out curse Bronagh Murphy, not even a sailor.

"I'm cleanin' windows, not performin' a stunt. All of ye', bar Keela, feck off."

"No can do, short stuff."

I wanted to look down and target my best glare in Alec's direction, but Ryder was right. I feared heights and that meant I couldn't look down. The only reason I was on the stupid ladder was because

Keela was in hardcore nesting mode, and she was very irritable, so I was doing what I could to help her relax at this stressful time.

"Come down," Damien asked, sounding closer. "*Please?*"

"I can do this, and the more you lot say I can't, the more I'm determined to clean the poxy window."

"Your handprint is gone, Lana," Keela cheered. "Ye' did it."

I smiled and dropped my ball of newspaper, letting it fall to the ground. I positioned myself to climb down, gripping the ladder tightly. Everything was going well until I accidentally looked down and froze.

"Oh, fuck," I shouted. "Are ye' *sure* this is just a three-story house? Feels a lot bloody higher from up 'ere."

"Don't look down!" everyone shouted in unison.

I couldn't focus on anything but the concrete ground that seemed to be swaying from side to side the longer I looked at it.

"I'm lookin' down," I screeched. "Oh, my *God*. I'm lookin' down!"

"Shit," Alec said. "This is bad."

"You all look like ants!" I swallowed. "Tiny ants."

Keela laughed but covered her mouth so I wouldn't hear her, but I heard her anyway.

"Why did ye' let me do this?" I snapped at her. "Why, Keela?"

"Because ye' wouldn't let *me* do it!"

"You're pregnant!" everyone chorused.

"Story of me bleedin' life."

"What is all the shoutin' about?"

"Branna," I squealed. "I can't move, and the ground is movin'."

"Oh, bollocks."

I could see Branna walk into Alec and Keela's garden out of the corner of my eye, and a tall figure followed her. I assumed that to be Ryder. When I heard babbling and soft crying, I knew they had the twins in their arms.

"I knew you'd get stuck up there," Damien informed me. "I'm gonna have to come and get you before gravity does."

Keela laughed. "He sounds like Marlin from *Finding Nemo*."

"You take that back because I'm *always* down for adventures. Just last night, Alannah and I were roughhousing and—"

"Okay!" I screeched, mortified that he would talk about our sex life so openly. "I'll come down. Just *stop talkin'*."

"If I knew kinky tales would have got your ass in gear"—Alec snickered—"I'd have gotten Damien over here sooner."

"Kiss me arse!"

"Can't," he answered. "Baby brother would hurt me."

"You bet your ass I would."

I closed my eyes and took each step very slowly. I listened to everyone's encouragement, and when I felt hands touch my hips, I just about died with relief.

"I'm *never* doin' that again," I said when my feet touched the ground. "That was horrible."

"I don't know why you got up there in the first place."

I stiffened. "Because Keela needed me to do it."

Damien sighed but said nothing further.

"Why aren't ye' in work?"

"The shop is slow today, so we took our break earlier than usual. Harley and Dante went out a while ago to get Gavin and we covered for them, so they've got it on lock until we come back."

"Hmmm."

"What does hmmm mean?"

"Nothin'," I replied. "It means nothin'."

I turned to Keela, who hugged me and thanked me profusely for helping her.

"I need a cup of tea," I announced. "Me nerves are *gone*."

Everyone chuckled as we entered Alec and Keela's house and, of course, headed for the kitchen. The lads got the bags of messages in, and once they were on the counters, myself and Keela began to empty them and put the food away. I felt Damien's eyes on me the entire time, but I ignored him as best as I could. I was angry with him over our fight, and I refused to pretend like it didn't happen.

"I read something interesting today."

I took Jules from Branna and snuggled him against my chest as I gave my attention to Alec.

"*You* know how to read?"

"Don't annoy me, dwarf. I'm in a good mood today."

"Fine, proceed."

"I read online this morning that the first thing a man notices about a woman and keeps his attention is ultimately the thing he can't live without."

"Did it give you statistics about what a man notices first?"

Alec grinned. "Of course."

He no doubt found it on the recommended section of Twitter.

"What's the first thing *you* think a man notices?"

"The first thing a man notices in a woman are her eyes."

I eyed him, wondering what was wrong with him.

"When her eyes aren't looking," he continued, "he notices her tits."

There's the man we all knew and love.

"You're so predictable."

"It's the truth." Alec shrugged, then looked at Damien. "Be honest, what did you notice about Alannah first?"

"Not her tits."

Alec rolled his eyes. "Her ass then."

Damien dimpled, and I blinked with surprise.

"I don't have a nice arse, though."

Gasps were sounded, and Damien looked like he was physically wounded.

"Don't say that," Branna warned. "When I said I didn't like mine, I got an hour-long lecture about it."

"I'm *still* upset with you for saying that," Ryder mumbled. "It's my favourite ass in the world."

I smiled and looked down at their son in my arms. I pretended to chew on Jules's fingers when he stuck them in my mouth, and he laughed.

"You're so perfect," I told him. "You and all your white hair."

When he looked up at me and smiled, my heart squeezed.

"Oh God, these twins look like duplicates of the big twins."

"The big twins." Keela snorted. "Is that what we're labellin' them as, big twins and little twins?"

"Nico and Damien can be Thing One and Thing Two," I said. "These precious boys can be called angels instead."

"Typical," Damien muttered.

I ignored him.

"I can't wait until I can babysit these two." I looked up at their parents. "*When* will that be?"

Ryder looked at Branna. "She wants to take them, so we should let her."

Alec laughed as his eagerness.

Branna hesitated. "What if I cry?"

"I'll hold you," Ryder answered. "I'll make it *all* better."

"I'm sure you will," I mumbled.

He grinned but kept his eyes on his wife.

"Okay." Branna nodded. "But we should start with them just being gone for a few hours. Not overnight yet."

"Sweetness, a few hours alone with you is all I need for us to experience heaven."

I blushed on Branna's behalf, and it amused Keela, who was watching me.

"I can take them for a few hours on Saturday," I suggested. "I have a free day from work, and Damien is home that day, too. He'll be drafted in if I need any help."

Damien agreed with a bob of his head.

"Sounds good to me," Ryder said and looked at his wife.

"Me too," Branna said. "Be warned, I bet I'll cry."

I chuckled, then turned to Alec. He had his arms around Keela with his hands on her baby bump.

"Since you mentioned readin', I just remember that *I* read somethin' on Twitter last night that will mind fuck ye'."

Alec locked eyes on me. "Hit me with it."

"The alphabet song is really just 'Twinkle, Twinkle, Little Star'."

I watched as Alec mumbled the two songs, and when the realisation dawned on him that they had the exact same melody, it cracked me up.

"How the hell have I not known this before now?" he asked Keela.

She shrugged. "I didn't know it until now either."

I watched as he tried to disprove my fact, and he couldn't.

"Ah!" He grunted. "Fuck you, Alannah."

I beamed.

"You enjoy your bickering so much it's actually scary."

I looked at Ryder. "It keeps me young."

Alec then announced he was making pancakes, and both Damien and Ryder were happy with the news.

"He is obsessed with makin' pancakes," Keela said to me. "It's his thing as of late."

"Not just any pancakes," Alec corrected. "The *perfect* pancakes."

"What *is* the perfect pancake?" I quizzed.

"I'm glad you asked."

Keela's shoulders slumped. "I'm not."

Alec ignored her and focused on me.

"The perfect pancake requires skill. Any moron can make a basic pancake, but it takes a true master to use his talent to execute the perfect circle of roundness, the right consistency of fluffiness, and of course, the correct ratio of golden brown."

I blinked. "I just pour the batter in the pan, wait till it bubbles, then I flip it."

Alec curled his lip up in disgust. "I expect nothing less from a rookie."

I rolled my eyes.

"Okay, pancake master. Make me one of these perfect pancakes."

"Your wish is my command."

He then proceeded to make a bunch of pancakes, and when he put one on a plate in front of me and handed me a fork, I cut off a piece and tasted it.

"Well, Lana, is it the perfect pancake?"

Alec leaned closer after Keela spoke and asked, "*Is* it?"

"I already regret sayin' this … but yeah, it is."

"Aha!" Alec shouted and spun to his fiancée. "I *told* you!"

"That was the hardest thing I have ever had to admit in me entire life."

Keela snorted. "It looked like it physically hurt ye' to say it."

"It did." I bobbed my head. "Like I swallowed acid."

Everyone chuckled but then quietly ate the pancakes Alec made. After we had all eaten, our conversation resumed.

"Do you think you'll become a dad today?" Ryder quizzed.

"No," Alec answered with a grunt. "The kid is too snug in there. I'm worried the baby will come when I'm not around. I've been thinking about how Keela can reach me if she can't find a phone, and I've come up with an idea."

I gave him my full attention.

"I can't wait to hear this."

He ignored me.

"Storm is untrainable," he began, "but Tyson isn't, so maybe I can train *him* to find *me* when Keela's water breaks."

"And how are you going to pull that off, Mystic Meg?"

"I'm talented," Alec stated, narrowing his eyes at me. "I can impart wisdom easily enough."

Bull. Shit.

"If you manage to train Tyson to find you when Keela's water breaks, I'll give you a hundred euros *and* call you Lord Alec for a whole month."

"Deal!"

We shook on it, and it amused everyone. The twins became restless then, so I handed Jules back to his parents, and the four of them returned home, leaving just me, Damien, Alec, and Keela in the kitchen. Alec and Keela were cuddling and being cute, whereas I wouldn't look at Damien even though I felt him staring at me. Alec noticed this and, of course, called us on it.

"Trouble in paradise?"

I snorted but said nothing.

"We're just fine," Damien said, his tone sarcastic. "Aren't we, baby?"

"Fuckin' dandy."

Keela blinked. "I love when you curse. I think it's sexy."

I grinned. "Fuck a duck."

"Stop it." She giggled.

"What can you two *possibly* argue about?" Alec asked. "You're still in the honeymoon stage."

"Oh, I think we jumped that ship a while ago." I snickered. "Right around the time Damien became a walkin' arsehole when he doesn't get his way. Isn't that right, Jack Frost?"

Keela widened her eyes at me, then flicked them to Damien behind me.

"Oh," she whispered. "This will end in angry sex."

"I can assure that it most definitely will n—*Damien*!"

"Yup." Alec snorted as I was twirled around, picked up, and tossed over Damien's shoulder before he stalked out of the room. "It most definitely *will* end in angry sex."

I smacked my fists on Damien's behind and shouted obscenities at him as he climbed the stairs of Alec and Keela's house. He brought us to the first guest bedroom, slammed the door behind us, and quite literally threw me onto the bed. I smacked my hands against the mattress in outrage, but before I could push myself into an upright position, Damien leaned over me and crushed his mouth against mine. He bit down on my lower lip, and when I opened my mouth to yelp, he plunged his tongue inside.

I was furious with him, but by God, I was so turned on by his forcefulness that I kissed him back with a raw hunger. He'd behaved this way only a handful of times, and it was always when we were fighting. This was what I liked to call *Damien fucking me into submission*. As he kissed me, he pushed my dress up, pulled my underwear from my body, and then busied himself with yanking down his own clothes.

"What did I tell you I was going to do to you whenever you caught an attitude with me?"

I licked my lips. "You said you'd fuck me."

"Yeah." Damien glared down at me. "I said I'd fuck you."

He moved down my body, and I cried out when his tongue lapped against my clit, before it slid lower and plunged into my pussy. He tongue fucked me until my eyes crossed and my hands fisted the bed sheets under me. When he removed his tongue from me, he replaced it with his cock. I opened my eyes and locked them on his as he pushed into me. We both moaned in unison. He wasn't gentle as his fingers bit painfully into the flesh of my thighs, and I didn't want him to be.

Damien loved me, but when he was angry, he fucked me like he hated me, and I loved every second of it.

Straight away, he thrust into me with hard, fast-paced strokes. I slammed my hand over my mouth when a cry climbed up my throat. I was very aware of whose house I was in, and I was trying to keep our lovemaking silent instead of confirming what Keela and Alec already knew we were doing, but Damien wouldn't allow it. He grabbed my hand, pulled it from my mouth, and pinned it to my side. He pounded into me, and I cried out in delight.

"Yes, harder!" I shouted. "*Fuck*!"

"Let them hear you," he growled. "Let them know *exactly* what I'm doing to you."

He leaned his head down to mine, and just when I thought he was going to kiss me, he dipped his head, brought his mouth to my neck, and he *bit* me. Not enough to break the skin, but enough for it to sting with pain. I hissed, but my body arched against Damien's, confusing the pain with pleasure. Everything happened rapidly then. Damien leaned back, then balancing himself on one arm, he removed his hand from my wrist and brought it to my pussy. He rubbed his thumb up and down before he rested it on my clit and swirled it around. My breath caught, and an orgasm began to build.

"Damien."

His eyes fluttered shut. "Again."

I groaned as he bucked into me, stealing my breath.

"Say it *again*!"

"Damien."

"Fu...*ck*." He licked his lower lip. "I'm gonna come."

He pinched my clit the second the words left his mouth, and the pain caused my orgasm to unexpectedly slam into me. A silent cry passed my lips as a pulse of ecstasy started at my clit and spread outward like scorching flames. The sensation wrapped around every muscle and drained me of energy. I hadn't realised that my eyes had closed, but when I blinked them open, Damien was already pulling out of my body. He retrieved my underwear as I pushed myself up to my elbows. He didn't speak a word to me as he slid them back up my shaking legs to my mid-thigh so I could pull them the rest of the way up.

"I didn't wear a rubber," he said. "You'll have to go to the bathroom so your panties don't get ruined."

I lay back on the bed in a sweaty mess and tried to remember if I took my pill that morning. I couldn't recall whether I did, and I inwardly kicked myself.

"I'm mortified."

"Why?"

"Why?" I repeated incredulously. "We aren't at home. We can't just have sex in your brother's house like it's okay."

"I told you about your attitude and what I was going to do if you had one with me."

I rolled my eyes. "I'm aware."

"You could have said no." He shrugged. "If you showed any sign of not wanting me, I wouldn't have touched you and you know it."

I gritted my teeth. "Ye' *know* I can't think straight when ye' start touchin' me."

My body acted of its own accord when Damien put his hands on me. Like a shark who caught the scent of blood, he needed to feed. When Damien touched me, I needed him to *never* stop touching me.

"Yeah," he replied, and I heard the smile in his tone. "I know."

I exhaled a breath.

"I'm still mad at ye' over our fight."

"And I'm still mad at you over it," Damien replied. "But don't for one second think I don't love you because I do. My brothers don't care if their women talk shit to them, but I do, so remember that when you want to run your mouth."

It was almost embarrassing how attractive I found him to be when he was domineering.

"Yeah." I grunted. "I got that message loud and clear, bossy hole."

He pulled me to my feet, and before I could fix my underwear and dress, Damien caught my chin with his fingers, tipped my head back, and pressed his lips to mine. He kissed me until my hands found their way up to his hair and tangled around the thick strands. My toes curled, and my body pressed against him before I realised I had moved. His arms were wrapped around my waist, and when we finally separated, my eyes were closed, and my breathing was laboured.

Damien, on the other hand, sounded perfectly fine.

"Ye' can't kiss me when I'm mad at ye'."

I opened my eyes just as he invaded my space.

"Fucking *watch* me."

I experienced a moment of déjà vu because I was sure he said something just as similar to me once before. Before he could dip his head and kiss me again, I backed away from him, keeping my eyes trained on his.

"I have to get cleaned up."

He rolled his eyes over me, then jerked his head as if to give me *permission* to go to the bathroom. When I narrowed my eyes, a delicious grin tugged at his plump lips. With my head held high, I turned and walked as best as I could with my underwear around my thighs to leave the bedroom and go into the bathroom. After relieving myself and cleaning up, I washed my hands and returned to the bedroom to find Damien had already remade the bed and had the room looking just as pretty as when we first entered.

"I have to go back to work," he said as he followed me down the stairs. "I'll be home in time for dinner."

"I'm not makin' ye' dinner," I told him. "Ye' can go to Branna if you're hungry; she'll feed ye'."

Damien sighed. "You'd really let me starve?"

"Yes, I would. Now, don't let the door hit ye' in the arse on the way out."

I jumped when he smacked my behind at the bottom of the stairs and glared at him over my shoulder as he left the house with a smirk on his face. When he was gone, I turned my attention to Alec and Keela who were arguing in the sitting room.

"I'm goin' to start a gang," Keela announced. "You'll see, playboy. And it'll be a *terrifyin'* gang!"

"You said book club wrong."

I found it ironic that Keela's weapon of choice turned out to be a book as she flung it at Alec's head at rapid speed. He tried to dodge it, bless him, but it clapped him in the centre of his chest.

"*Harry Potter*," he rasped when he looked at the book's cover. "Why does it always have to be *Harry Potter*?"

I know the answer, I thought merrily. *They were the biggest books Keela owned and would do the most damage.*

"I thought ye' loved *Harry Potter*," I commented as I leaned my shoulder against the doorway. "Isn't that why ye' became a banshee over that stupid cup?"

"How *dare* you call it stupid!" Alec shouted in outrage as he jumped to his feet and spun to face me. "It was perfect, and you broke it because you're *evil*."

I loved him so much that it wasn't even funny. He was honestly my favourite person ... but he wasn't allowed to know that.

I looked at Keela. "Phone me if you go into labour. I'm goin' over to Branna's house for a bit to leave ye' both ... to whatever this is."

"Sure," Alec hollered as I left. "Have angry sex in our guest room with my baby brother, then up and leave. Rude ass!"

My cheeks burned with heat as I left the house and crossed the road to Branna and Ryder's house. Ryder was backing out of his garden in his work truck with Damien in the passenger side. Three teenage boys wearing my old school's uniform were walking by just as I stepped onto the path, and one of them looked at me and stopped dead in his tracks, causing his other two friends to slow down.

"Fuck me," he said, his eyes wide. "You're *seriously* good lookin'."

I wished I could have disappeared into thin air.

My lips parted. "Uh, thank you."

"Can I get a selfie with ye'?" he asked. "Our teacher gave us an assignment to pose with someone who we thought was beautiful, and that, missus, is *you*."

I wanted to run away, but I couldn't.

"Okay."

I was like a fish out of water when this kid, who was taller than me, cosied up to my side, put his arm around my waist, and held his phone out. His friends didn't seem at all bothered, like their friend stopping a stranger, complimenting them, and then asking for a picture was a regular part of their day.

"Smile."

We both smiled as he took the picture.

"Seriously good lookin'," he muttered to himself.

When he turned to look down at me, he looked over my head first and jumped back.

"Christ," the kid yelped. "Ye' scared the shite outta me, man."

Before I could turn around, *he* said, "Is there a reason you were touching *my* girl, kid?"

Oh. Shite.

I turned to face him. "He is just bein' nice, Dame."

"Yeah, man," the kid echoed me. "I wasn't bein' rude. I just told 'er how good lookin' she is."

"What's with the picture bullshit?"

"It's a school assignment. We have to—"

"Try again."

The kid's friends snickered as he froze to the spot.

"Okay," he said, nervously. "I have a bet on with a mate at school. We have to see which one of us can get the most pictures with hot women. We get bonus points if they kiss us."

I gasped. "Ye' little fecker."

The kid looked at me and grinned. "Sorry, but ye' *are* beautiful. That wasn't a lie."

"Get lost," Damien growled, "before I put my foot up your ass."

All three of the teens fled, and I was left staring after them with my lips parted.

"What just happened?"

"What just happened was you're too trusting of people."

I turned to Damien and frowned. "He just wanted a picture, *and* he called me beautiful."

"How can you *not* see when guys lust over you?"

"Because he was a child who wasn't lustin' over me maybe?"

"I could sense his thoughts with just one glance at him," Damien said. "He thought you were a hell of a lot more than beautiful."

I placed my hands on my hips. "Why did ye' get out of the truck?"

ALANNAH

"Because three teenagers stopped you and one was eye fucking you," he replied with a raised brow. "You expect me to just *let* that happen?"

I laughed. "You're so … so..."

"So *what*?"

"Protective."

Damien relaxed. "Because I love you."

"I know. I love ye' too … but I'm still mad at ye'"

He leaned down and kissed me. "I'm still mad at you too."

When he turned and jogged back towards the truck, Ryder was staring at me, and when he shouted, "Alannah, you're so beautiful, will you take a picture with me?" I stuck my middle finger up at him in response. He laughed as I continued my journey into the house. Branna, being the super mother that she was, had already settled both twins in their nursery and was tiptoeing down the stairs as I closed the front door behind me.

"I was goin' to help ye' with the babies."

"No need." She smiled. "They're great sleepers."

That they were. I followed Branna into the kitchen and sat down at the table. She flipped the kettle on and placed a baby monitor on the counter so she could keep an eye on her sons. I filled her in on what happened to me out front with the teenagers, and she thought it was the funniest thing since sliced bread.

"It's you, me, and a cup of tea."

I hummed. "Tea makes everythin' better."

I thanked her as she made me a cup and set it down in front of me.

"Ye've got that right," she said, exhaling a breath as she plonked down on the chair with her own cup in front of her.

My lips twitched. "Ye' seem tired."

"I'm fuckin' knackered."

"I was serious earlier when I said I'd babysit the twins. When they're bigger, I'll babysit overnight whenever you and Ry want. I love kids. I take Georgie one night a week for Nico and Bee, and I

53

have Jax and Locke tomorrow night for Kane and Aideen."

"You're insane," Branna said with a shake of her head. "I mean that in the nicest way possible."

I giggled. "Thanks, I guess."

"I know I said earlier that I'll cry, and I know that I will when ye' take them, but me and Ryder *need* this break you're givin' us on Saturday. Our lads are great babies, but we need this alone time together. Havin' quickies is the best we can do right now. I felt awful for Ry this mornin'. We were havin' sex, and just as we were gettin' into it, Jules screamed bloody murder to be fed. I got me rocks off, but Ry didn't."

I cringed. "I'll take them for the whole day, so ye' can have sex the entire time with no interruptions."

"Thanks." Branna chuckled. "Ye' have no idea how much we're lookin' forward to stayin' in bed all day."

I could imagine.

"How long do ye' have left on your maternity leave?"

"Three more months," she answered. "I miss it so much, but when I think of leavin' the boys, I get so down."

"Will ye' reduce your hours when ye' go back?"

"I can't because we need both incomes now that we have the twins," she explained. "I've done a few shifts over the past few weeks, just to test meself with the boys in the crèche set up for the staff. I honestly don't know what I'd do if I couldn't bring them to work with me and check on them whenever I want to."

"You're lucky," I said. "Aideen would *kill* for that, but at least Kane's job doesn't require him to actually leave the apartment, so she knows the boys are in good hands with 'im while she's not there."

Branna nodded in agreement.

"Tell me to fuck off if I'm oversteppin' 'ere," she began, "but did I notice some tension between you and Damien at Alec and Keela's?"

I took a sip of my tea.

"Branna, ye' don't know the *half* of it." I sighed, settling into the chair. "Let me tell ye' about how much that white-haired fucker has irritated me so far today."

CHAPTER FIVE

A half an hour after I entered Branna's house, Kane showed up with Jax and Locke while Aideen was at work. A half an hour after *they* showed up, Nico, Bronagh, and Georgie stopped by. When Alec came over, any semblance of peace was completely gone out the door with his big mouth. Luckily, the twins, Nixon and Jules, could sleep through anything, so not even Alec Slater could ruin their nap.

"Where's Keela?"

"At home," he answered as he fell into the chair next to me. "I saw the kids arrive and wanted to come over and play with them, but she wants me to play with *her,* and I refuse to. I'm too scared my cock head will hit my *kid's* head if I have sex with her."

"Alec!" I screeched. "Too much information!"

Nico laughed, Kane's lips twitched, and the sisters giggled.

"You're so fucking cute." Alec snickered. "You have loud, angry sex with Damien in my guest bedroom, but I can't say cock head without you—"

I dived on him, grabbed his earlobes with my fingers, and pulled on them until he was a hollering mess.

"Mercy," he yelled. "Mercy, woman!"

I released his ears and slid back onto my chair, ignoring the cries of laughter from around us.

"Now," I said as I straightened my dress. "Keep it PG."

"You're a violent little midget!" Alec hissed as he rapidly rubbed his ears.

I glared at him. "Remember that the next time you want to air me business in public."

"It's my *guest bedroom* I need to air. The smell of sex is—"

Alec cut himself off when I jumped at him again; only this time, he had the good sense to cover his ears. The eejit forgot to guard his nipples, though, and I made him pay dearly for that error in judgment. I latched onto them and tweaked them both so hard I knew I'd probably leave bruises. Alec roared, and the kids screamed back at him, thinking he was playing a game. Nico was laughing so hard he had to sit down on the floor, and Kane looked like he had tears in his eyes from laughter. I couldn't see the sisters, but I heard their wheezing as they laughed.

"Mercy!"

When I let go of Alec this time, he covered his nipples with his hands, bent forward until his forehead touched the table and groaned in pain.

"I think they're bleeding!" He croaked. "Oh, merciful God, I think you twisted them right off."

I rolled my eyes.

"You're like a hobbit on steroids!" he continued. "I never knew you possessed such strength. Christ."

I began to worry about him then as he did look to be in a lot of pain.

"Let me see—"

"You have done *enough* damage," he cut me off before he looked at his brothers. "Lotion. I need lotion for my nipples."

Nico slapped his hand against his thigh, Kane covered his eyes with his palms as his shoulders shook, and Bronagh and Branna were all but crying with laughter. I stood, placed my hands on my hips, and stared at Alec.

"Let me see."

With a scowl, he got to his feet, pulled up his top, and my eyes paused on his abs instead of his nipples. Alec was insanely attractive, but I was not attracted *to* him. I loved him like a brother, but there was no denying that the man had a body and face that would cause both sexes to stop and stare.

"I'm telling Damien that you checked me out," Alec warned. "Look at you, practically drooling."

My lips twitched as I stepped closer and peered at his nipples.

"They're still attached."

"They're throbbing," he grunted. "And *not* in a good way."

I lifted my hands and flattened my palms against his nipples, and he hissed.

"If you ever need another job," he said to me, "you should consider applying to Helga's house of pain."

I smiled as I dropped my hands and stared up at him.

"Ye'll be fine, you big baby."

"The only way I'll forgive you is if I get to twist *your* nipples, too."

Nico spluttered with laughter. "Damien will *murder* you."

Alec grinned. "Worth it."

"Ye'll *never* see me nipples."

"They're probably weird looking nipples anyway, so maybe I'm better off."

When all the excitement and laughter died down, Branna and Bronagh decided to do laps around the back garden in hopes to kick-start Bronagh's labour. Jax and Georgie went with them while I went into the sitting room with the lads and Locke. He clung to me like a spider monkey, and it amused his father.

"My boys adore you."

"I know," I said proudly. "I don't blame them, though. I'm pretty amazin'."

The lads snorted.

"Ye' should go over to Keela," I said to Alec. "She's probably gonna try to clean the ceilin' or somethin' if you aren't there to watch 'er."

"But she said I could come over here."

"Sayin' it and meanin' it are two different things."

Nico bobbed his head in agreement. "I've already covered this in chapter one. Consult your book if you forgot."

Alec leaned his head back against the sofa.

"I can't deal with none of your Man Bible preaching today, Dominic. Keela said it was cool to come over here, so I'm *staying*."

Nico looked out the sitting room window and froze.

"Bro."

"No," Alec said. "I'm staying here."

"Shut the fuck up and look over at your house."

To appease him, Alec turned and looked over his shoulder but instantly froze as well. Curiosity got the better of me, so I leaned forward and looked out the window, too. I tensed when I saw a figure standing in the sitting room window of Alec and Keela's house staring over at the house.

I widened my eyes. "Is that *Keela*?"

"If it's not," Alec murmured, "I need to call Ed and Lorraine Warren to exorcise my damn house."

"If ye' manage to get hold of Ed on the phone, get the number for the ghostbusters next 'cause he's been dead for years."

Alec didn't look away from Keela, who was still staring over at us.

"Since you find this so funny, Lana, why don't *you* go over and see if she is okay?"

"Why?" I grinned at the back of his head. "Are you too scared?"

"Fucking terrified," he answered.

I laughed, Nico grinned, and Kane shook his head as he took Locke from me.

"These are the rantings of a madman," I said to Nico. "Right?"

"You can just say Alec. It's another term for madman."

I bumped fists with him and chuckled.

"I'm fucking delighted that you're both finding this funny, but I swear to God that Keela just made the sign of the cross and pointed over at me. What the *fuck* does that mean?"

"Maybe it means she's plannin' on you meetin' God sooner than you think," I teased.

"That does it!" Alec announced suddenly and loudly. "I'm not leaving this damn house. Alannah, go over and make sure Keela is okay. And Nico?"

"Yeah?"

"Lock the door behind her."

I laughed harder than I had in a long time, and I practically skipped out of the house and across the road. When I entered Alec and Keela's, I walked into the sitting room and said to Keela, "Ye' have Alec terrified that you're possessed."

"I *knew* I'd scare 'im by just standin' 'ere."

"Come with me." I chuckled. "Alec thinks the house needs to be exorcised."

With a laugh, Keela and I left her house and made our way over to Branna's.

"All is well," I announced. "She just wanted to freak the man-child out."

"I resent that," Alec said, drawing a grin from me as he focused on Keela. "Why did you say I could come over here if you didn't really want me to?"

Keela shrugged. "I wanted to see if ye' could figure it out your-self."

"Clearly, I can't."

"I just find it interestin' how—"

"Retreat."

Keela stopped speaking to listen to Nico mutter to Alec.

"What?"

"It's a trap."

Alec looked confused. "How?"

"She doesn't find anything interesting; it's a trap. She's closing in on your fuckup."

"But you said it's only when she says, 'I find it funny,' that it's a trap."

"Funny. Interesting. Either word is lethal."

Alec groaned. "I can't keep up with all these stupid rules." He looked at Keela. "I'm so sorry for leaving when you didn't want me to. I won't do it again, just please don't make me spend the next eight hours wondering how I can make it up to you while you ignore me. *Please*. I can't deal with it."

He sounded like he was going to have a nervous breakdown.

"Honey, stop." Keela frowned. "It's okay."

I blinked.

"Son of a bitch," said Nico. "You just cheated the system."

"What?" Alec asked.

"You broke down like a bitch ... but it worked. She's not mad at you no more." Nico shook his head. "Bro, new chapter to The Man Bible."

That fecking Man Bible.

Alec ignored his brother and focused on Keela.

"I lust you," he practically growled at her.

Keela grinned. "I lust ye', too."

I looked back and forth between them.

"What the hell was that about?"

Keela laughed. "When he is hot for me, his new thing is to tell me he lusts me."

I looked at Alec, who was still watching Keela with hungry eyes.

"You're like a dog in heat."

Keela snickered as Alec turned his gaze towards me. Slowly.

"You're a plague," he told me.

I smiled a toothy grin.

"Upon *your* house," I finished.

Alec rolled his eyes. "You were definitely put on this Earth to mess with me."

"I'm serving me purpose well then, bitch."

I screamed like a banshee when he suddenly lunged at me, wrapped an arm around my neck, and pulled until I was bent at the waist. I gripped his arm with one hand, then fisted his shirt with the other.

"Alec!" I screamed with laughter. "Don't even *think*—"

I cut myself off screaming when he gave me a noogie. I tried to break his hold but couldn't, so I used the only weapon I had. My teeth. I chopped down on Alec's forearm, and he yelped and released me instantly.

"She bit me!" he stated, then to me, he said, "You *bit* me!"

"Ye' squeezed me so tight me boobs were about to pop."

Alec's eyes dropped to my chest, and I instantly threw my hands up in the air.

"*Really?*"

He grinned, his eyes returning to mine. "You mentioned them."

"There is somethin' *really* wrong with you."

"You say that like it's new information."

I shook my head and grabbed Keela's hand.

"Let's join Bran and Bee out back," I said, tugging her out of the room. "I need ye' to have your demon spawn today just to start Alec's turmoil for the next eighteen years."

"A plague!" he shouted after us. "You are a *plague*!"

And that was Alec Slater basically declaring his love for me.

CHAPTER SIX

Two days later...

"**W**hat do ye' think the doctor is goin' to say?"

My da squeezed my hand tightly. "It'll be good news."

I stared at him. "What if it's not?"

"It can't be anythin' other than good news," Da replied, his voice tight with emotion. "She can't be anythin' other than healthy. Not after what she's been through. Life can't be that cruel."

I wanted to tell him that life didn't care what you had been through; it put bumps in the road no matter what turn you took.

I leaned my head on my da's shoulder and closed my eyes. I'd felt sick from the moment I woke up that morning. It had nothing to do with my ongoing fight with Damien and everything to do with my mother. Today, we found out the results of her mammogram. We would find out if her cancer was gone, or if she needed more treatment to get rid of it. Me and my da were nervous wrecks, and we had just one another to lean on. My ma asked that it just be the three of us at this appointment, so that meant Damien wasn't here for me. Our stupid fight was still ongoing, but he intended to come with me to the hospital until I told him what my ma wanted.

He went to work instead and told me to call him when I found out the news. I prayed to God that when I did that, I would have something good to tell him. We had been in the hospital for a whole hour waiting to talk to the professor who headed the medical team assigned to my ma during her whole cancer ordeal, and when she entered his office just for a few minutes by herself, we were left feeling very uneasy. She said she wanted to ask him some private questions before we all went in to hear the results. I remained seated outside with my da as they disappeared into the room, and when we looked at one another after five long minutes, we stood at the exact same time.

Something wasn't right.

We both started for the door of the doctor's office, and we entered it without knocking or announcing ourselves. My heart stopped beating and my hand latched onto my da's forearm when I saw that my ma was sitting in front of the doctor's desk … in tears.

"No," I said outlaid. "No, please. *No.*"

My ma jerked her gaze to the doorway when she heard me, and when she saw us, she smiled, though she was still sobbing.

"I'm cancer *free!*"

For a few seconds, no one moved, spoke, or even breathed. Then, like the snap of my fingers, I screamed and rushed at my ma. I heard nothing but the sound of my own heartbeat in my ears. When I wrapped my arms around her, I hadn't realised I was crying until my lungs told me to take a breath. I felt my da's arms wrap around us. Both he and my ma were talking over each other, and they cried and laughed at the same time.

When we separated, I placed my hands on either side of my head in disbelief.

"This doesn't feel real," I said. "I prayed for this, begged God for this."

"It's real, sweetie."

"Ma!" I scowled. "We were supposed to be *with* you when ye' found out."

"I know, but honey, I wanted to know first in case it was bad, so

I could be aware and could comfort you and Daddy."

I blinked. "If it was bad news, comfortin' *us* isn't what you should be doin'."

"You and your da come first." She shrugged. "Always have and will."

I leaned in and pressed my forehead against hers.

"You're better."

Her arms came around my waist. "I'm better, bear."

When I cried once again, it was to my mother's musical laughter. It took a further five minutes of hugging, crying, and laughing before we settled down in front of the professor. I listened as best as I could as he repeated my ma's test results to us. She was cancer free; her surgery and radiation had been successful, and no cancerous cells were left inside her breast.

The professor went into detail about how the mammogram worked, and how accurate the result was. When we left his office, it was after we had set up an appointment for my ma to return in one year for another mammogram. Once the cancer stayed away, she only required yearly tests.

I felt like I was floating, like everything was too perfect for it to be real. As my da drove us home, I phoned Damien.

"Hey," he answered on the second ring. "What happened?"

"She's better," I said. Closing my eyes, I scarcely believed the words. "The results show no cancer. She's better."

"Baby, I'm so happy for her, for you, and your dad."

"I can't believe it," I said. "I really didn't think this would be the news we were goin' to receive. She's one of the lucky ones, Dame."

After I phoned Damien, I phoned Bronagh, who screamed and cried, triggering more tears to fall from my eyes. Once I assured her I'd come over to her house soon, I got off the phone with her and spent the next few hours at my parents' house. Together with my ma and da, we had lunch and then a really long conversation about the future and how it was wide open and ours for the taking. When my da dropped me to Bronagh's house, I felt lighter than I had felt in months. Bronagh tackled me with a hug when she opened the door, then dragged me into the kitchen where I filled her in on my ma's hospital appointment.

"Alannah, I'm so happy for 'er," she beamed. "So, *so* happy."

I smiled. "Me too, Bee."

She sighed, long and deep.

"Nothin' will top what ye' just told me, but do you know that Alec has been trainin' Tyson? Whenever liquid hits the floor, he has to come and find 'im. He said he's doin' it so if Keela goes into labour around 'im, he'll alert Alec to the scene. Keela has been pupsittin' Tyson the past two days because of it."

"Yeah, I know. We made a bet about it."

"I don't even *wanna* know." Bronagh snorted.

"Are *you* havin' any signs of labour?" I asked. "If you were, it would be the cherry on top of a perfect day."

"I felt some pains this mornin', but nothin' since, so I've no idea."

I got excited.

"Do some jumpin' jacks or squats. It might help."

"If I squat around Dominic, he'll get grouchy because he'll want to touch me, but he knows we can't have sex 'cause he hurts me too much."

"Tell the big baby it's to get the little baby out, and he'll just have to suck it up."

Bronagh chuckled. "I'll pass it on."

My phone rang just as the kettle boiled.

"Hello?"

"Houston, we're havin' a baby."

"*What?*"

"Me water broke."

"Keela!" I gasped, startling Bronagh and Georgie. "Your water broke? Where is Alec?"

Bronagh clapped her hands together in delight, and Georgie copied her.

"He just got in from work. Me and Tyson were in the sittin' room, and out of nowhere a huge gush of water that I couldn't control just ruined the bloody settee. Tyson started barkin' and ran from the room and got Alec who had just pulled onto the driveway. The man has unpacked and repacked the hospital bag twice just to make sure we have everythin'." Keela chuckled. "He is in full-on daddy mode. I can barely get 'im to focus on me for more than two seconds."

"What will we do?" I asked, unsure. "I'm freakin' out."

"Branna is headin' to the hospital to be the lead midwife on me delivery. I already called 'er. She told us to come to the hospital and go from there. Aideen is meetin' us there since she's gonna be there for the birth as well. Alec will keep you all updated. I promise."

"Babe!" I squealed. "You're gonna be a mammy!"

"I know!" she said, her voice cracking. "I can't believe it. I got some pains an hour ago, and now me water has broke. It's movin' so fast!"

"Wish 'er good luck for me," Bronagh said, gaining my attention. "Tell her I love 'er."

"Bronagh says good luck, and that she loves you. I love you, too."

"I love ye' both, too," Keela said, then groaned. "I have to go. I have a pain, but Alec will keep you updated."

After I hung up the phone, I looked at Bronagh and said, "Alec and Keela are about to have a *baby*!"

"I can't believe it," Bronagh gushed. "I can't wait to see them with a baby of their own. They've been tryin' since Aideen was pregnant with Jax."

I covered my mouth with my hand.

"This is unreal," I said. "I'm so excited."

"This leaves Damien as the only Slater brother who isn't a daddy."

My smile slowly slid from my face, and Bronagh's eyes widened.

"I didn't mean it like *that*, I swear. I just mean it in a 'four down, one to go' kind of way."

I focused on Georgie. "I know what ye' mean. It's okay."

"Alannah"—she sighed—"I'm sorry."

"Don't be sorry," I said. "I know Damien wants kids with me. It's not news."

"He just sees his brothers expandin' their families and wants that experience too."

"I know." I nodded. "And it makes me feel like shite because I want that too, and I don't know if holdin' off is doin' anyone any good. I mean, what am I waitin' for?"

"You're waitin' for the right time."

"I don't think there ever is a right time to have babies."

Bronagh didn't reply, and she was saved by Nico when he entered the house. He was just as excited as we were when we told him Alec and Keela's news, and he nearly squeezed me to death when I told him my ma's news. He phoned Damien to let him know about their brother and Keela, and I felt even worse because I should have been the one to make that call. Bronagh went to take a nap not long after Nico came home, and Georgie went with her, rubbing her eyes with her tiny hand.

"What's wrong?"

I looked up at Nico when he spoke.

"What?"

"Something's wrong, so tell me what it is."

I hesitated. "It's nothin'."

"Alannah."

"It's just this stupid fight I'm havin' with Damien. It's been goin' on for two days. This is the longest fight we've ever had."

I filled Nico in on what we argued about, and he remained silent as I spoke.

"He doesn't get that I'm worried about rushin' things." I

frowned as I picked invisible dirt from under my nails. "I just ... I don't even know what to think because I *want* to get married and have babies, but somethin' in me mind makes me pause."

"Talking is what you guys need to do."

"I tried that," I huffed. "He started the fight and left for work."

"That was a dick move on his part, and I'm sure he knows that."

"I guess." I sighed.

Bronagh called for Nico to help her get comfortable in bed, and I used it as an excuse to take my leave. I walked back to my apartment building, enjoying another hot day. Instead of going up to my apartment, I got into my car and scrolled through some new emails. I opened an email from IKEA to read through their latest offers, and my eyes went wide when I saw the sale they had on art supplies. As well as the new shipments of supplies, they had restocked others. I usually went to my local craft store to get my supplies, but when IKEA had deals on, I took notice.

Always.

That email decided what I was going to do while I waited on news of Keela and Alec's baby. I put my car in gear and drove towards the bypass. It took twenty minutes, but eventually, I merged with traffic on the motorway. I turned up the volume on my radio and bopped along. Just as Celine Dion was about to slay bitches everywhere with her high note in "The Power of Love", my car jerked mid-drive.

For a moment, I thought I was in the wrong gear, but when I checked, I noted that I wasn't. I gripped the steering wheel when the car jerked again, then out of nowhere, smoke came from the bonnet of my car, and the engine made an awful chugging noise. Instantly, I signalled to the left. Pulling into the breakdown lane, I flipped my hazard lights on when I came to a stop.

"Ye've *got* to be jokin' me!"

I tried to start the car again, and nothing happened.

"Fuck!" I shouted and thumped the steering wheel. "Fuck, fuck, *fuck*!"

This was the last straw with this piece of shite car. It had cost me nothing but money fixing its many issues over the past two years, and I was *done*. I had earned enough money to buy a different car, something a lot smaller if I wanted a newer model, but anything would be better than the piece of shite Ford I currently owned. I got my phone from my bag and dialled Ryder Slater's mobile number.

"Alannah?"

"Ryder?"

"No, it's me."

Damien.

I wasn't surprised to hear his voice and dumbly asked, "Why're ye' answerin' your brother's phone?"

"Why are you *calling* my brother's phone?"

His tone irked me.

"Because you're an eejit, and I don't wanna speak to ye'."

He snorted. "Fine … here, *you* deal with her attitude."

If one of us had an attitude, it was *him*.

"Thanks," Ryder grunted. "Asshole."

Silence.

"Hey, Alannah banana."

That silly nickname he had recently taken to calling me made me feel like a little kid. I pretended that I found it annoying, but I secretly thought it was cute. I think Ryder knew that, so he kept on calling me it.

I sighed. "Hey, Ry."

"What did my pigheaded baby brother do to annoy you?"

"Oh, nothin', he just threw a tantrum that would rival Georgie, Jax, Locke, and the twins put together."

"Well, fuck a duck."

"My thoughts exactly."

He chuckled. "What's up, kid?"

"Me car broke down on the motorway. It made this really angry chuggin' noise, then the engine just gave out. I'm sittin' in the breakdown lane and don't know what to do."

"Which exits are you between?"

"Ten and eleven goin' northbound on the M50."

"We'll get to you in about twenty minutes ... maybe thirty, depending on the traffic. Okay?"

"Okay," I answered. "Did ye' know that Keela was in labour?"

"Yup," he replied, popping the P. "Branna called me, and Nico called Damien. Branna just checked on the twins in the daycare unit at the hospital, so she'll be able to be on shift to deliver their baby."

I pressed my hand against my chest. "I'm so happy she's doin' it."

"Me too," Ryder answered, then muffled shouting could be heard in the background. "I gotta go, kid. We'll be with you soon."

He hung up before I could reply. I sat in my car for ten minutes before the heat became too much so I popped the bonnet before I got out of the car, lifted it up and propped the stick thingy in place to keep it open. I placed my hands on my hips and stared at the engine. Other than some lingering smoke and the intense heat of the machine, nothing seemed out of place. Not to me anyway. I moved to my right when I heard a car pull up behind mine. I knew it was too fast to be Ryder, so I wasn't surprised when I found a tall, middle-aged man approaching me with a friendly smile.

"Car trouble?"

"Yeah." I nodded. "I'm not sure what the problem is, but I've called roadside rescue to get it sorted."

"Let me have a look for ye'," he said. "I'm Peter, by the way."

"Alannah."

Before I could say another word, the man rounded on me, his elbow brushing my arm as he passed me. He focused on my engine, and I moved around to keep an eye on him. We talked back and forth for what seemed like an eternity, and the entire time, he asked me if he could give me a lift anywhere to which I replied with a firm no.

"Honestly," I said to the man, feeling uncomfortable, "I'm really okay. Like I've said, I called roadside rescue and—"

Both myself and the man looked over our shoulders when a horn sounded. I was relieved to see the tow truck sporting the C.A.R. logo for Collins Auto Repair approaching us before pulling in front of my car in the breakdown lane and rolling to a complete stop. I should have been surprised when Damien got out of the driver's side of the truck, but I wasn't. I watched as he approached us, and I cursed at how attractive I found him in dirty work clothes when I wanted to remain angry with him for being a shitebag.

"Hey, baby," he greeted me before glancing at the man next to me. "What's up?"

Peter glanced at me. "Baby?"

I nodded. "He's me boyfriend."

"Oh." He nodded, his shoulders slumping slightly. "It looks like you don't need me help after all, Alannah."

I had told him that multiple times, but who was counting?

"No, man," Damien said as looked at my engine. "I've got her."

Peter cleared his throat, then bid us a farewell before he jogged back to his car. I waved at him as he drove by and merged with the motorway traffic, disappearing amongst the cars. When I turned back to Damien, he was already at work, so I moved to his side.

"You made a new friend, I see."

I scowled. "He just stopped to help me."

"He was looking at your ass."

"He was most likely lookin' at the car, Damien."

"He was looking at your ass," he repeated. "I saw him."

"Well, if he was, what was I supposed to do about it? I told 'im I didn't need help, and that I called roadside rescue. He was just bein' nice."

Damien snorted. "He *nicely* wanted a piece of ass."

I grunted. "Stop talkin' about *my* arse, and arses in general, okay? Great, thank you."

"But I love your ass in general."

"Yeah, well, love it from afar. You won't be seein' or touchin' it for a while."

"Not while you have this stick up it."

"You're *such* a dickhead," I quipped. "Go away. Make Ryder or one of the other lads come back and help me."

Damien rolled his head on his shoulders before he lifted his arm and rested it against the open bonnet. My eyes lingered on the bulge of his bicep for a moment too long, and when I flicked my gaze to Damien, I found a roguish grin on his too handsome face. I schooled my features, trying not to be embarrassed that he caught me checking him out.

"When one of the guys' girls call in a problem, they deal with it personally. You're *my* girl, so I deal with you. That's just the way it is in the shop."

"That may be the way it is in the shop, but do I look like I give a shite? Make Ryder or Gavin come and help me. I can't tolerate ye' when you're bein' like this."

"Like what?"

"Like *this*," I snapped. "Pissed off because ye' didn't get your way so you throw a tantrum."

Damien laughed, shook his head, then laughed some more before he turned back to my car, closed the bonnet, then moved back to his truck.

"It's broken," I said, keeping my arms crossed. "Smoke came from somewhere in there, and it made horrible noises."

"I'll bring it back to the shop and have JJ look at it with me. Go hop in the truck while I get it hooked up."

I frowned.

"What?"

"Nothin'."

Damien stared down at me, and when I rolled my eyes, I could have sworn I saw his lips twitch.

"I was on me way to IKEA," I explained. "I got an email about new art supplies. They're sellin' canvasses, *ten* different sizes, for half the price when you buy them in bundles. They even have pre-stretched ones back in stock, so I don't have to stretch them meself anymore. And me oil and acrylic paints are thirty percent off. They restocked me pencils and have this new brush I wanna try out *so* bloody bad. Now I can't go 'cause this stupid car is bein' extra stupid today."

Damien raised a brow.

"What?" I furrowed my brows. "You asked."

"Can you order them online?"

"Yeah," I grumbled. "But I like gettin' them in person."

"Until your car is fixed, you don't have a choice."

I grunted, then without a word, I walked towards the passenger side of the truck. I reached up to open the door, but before I could touch it, Damien reached over me and opened the door for me. He put his hands on my hips and lifted me up until my foot touched the third step. He closed the door behind me, so I buckled myself in and waited a few minutes while he hooked up my car and reeled it on the bed of the truck. I fanned myself with my hand, and by the time Damien got into the truck and started the engine, I was dying for some air conditioning.

"You look pretty," he commented as he merged into the traffic of the motorway.

I folded my arms under my chest.

"Thank you."

Silence.

I glanced at Damien's hands on the steering wheel and noticed how tight his grip was.

"Has Alec phoned anyone with an update?"

"Not yet," he answered coolly.

I looked out the window and set my jaw.

"Does your attitude mean I'm on the couch tonight again?"

"You bet your arse it does."

Damien grumbled to himself but said nothing further to me. We got caught in traffic, and it didn't help either of our moods. I couldn't believe when my stomach grumbled thirty minutes into the traffic jam.

"I can't believe I'm hungry," I said out loud. "I ate me weight durin' breakfast."

"I'm hungry too," Damien grunted. "It's times like this when I miss Wendy's."

I jerked my attention to Damien. "Who the *fuck* is Wendy?"

It took promptly zero seconds for Damien to erupt with laughter.

"It's a ... fast food place," he said while gasping from his laughter. "Not a woman."

I scowled at him but couldn't help but feel a huge amount of relief.

"I love it when you're jealous."

I looked out the window. "Shut up."

"You know you have no need to be, though," Damien continued. "This dick and heart are entirely yours."

"Ye' spend too much time with Alec," I said, my lips twitching. "Ye' sound more like 'im every single day."

"That's not a bad thing."

"We'll see."

Twenty more minutes in the gridlock nightmare, and I was irritated by everything.

"Damien!" I growled, feeling his eyes on me once again. "Stop lookin' at me."

"Can't help it. I visually enjoy you. I love you."

I knew he loved me, and I knew how much he wanted to spend his life with me. As I stared at Damien's side profile, I thought back to my conversation with Bronagh from two days ago, and one thing repeated in my mind. I *wanted* a marriage and children with Damien, so once again, I had to ask myself ... *what the hell am I waiting for?*

CHAPTER SEVEN

A bouncing baby boy.

After just three and a half hours of active labour, Alec and Keela were the proud parents of a beautiful baby boy who weighed seven pounds even and was twenty inches long. That was as much information as Branna had given me, Damien, and Ryder as we crowded around my phone to listen to the news in the garage. I screamed and jumped up and down with delight; Ryder and Damien hugged and patted the hell out of each other's back. Ryder gave me a squeeze, then Damien got his hands on me and held me so tight I felt his happiness deep in my bones.

"You're an uncle," I beamed. "Again."

"And you're an aunt again."

"Auntie," I jokingly corrected. "Oh, I want to see 'im *so* bad."

"Me too," he said and checked the clock on the wall. "It's only four ten ... How long do we have to wait for visiting hours?"

"Six, I think." I groaned. "That's gonna take *forever*."

I looked down at my phone when it pinged, and I screamed when I saw the first picture of Alec, Keela, and their stunning son.

"He's a *redhead*!" I gushed. "Look at all his hair! Slater babies do *not* come out of the womb bald!"

Ryder and Damien stared at the picture.

"Look at how happy he is," Ryder commented softly. "I never

thought I'd see him so complete."

My heart warmed. "He has his family."

Damien gave me a squeeze, and I knew he wanted what Alec had, what Ryder had, and what his other brothers had. A family. Children. A marriage. I wanted that too, and the longer this day carried on, Damien's and my relationship being rushed didn't seem as big of a problem as it did two days ago.

"He's gorgeous," I said, staring at the baby. "He looks so much like both of them ... but that hair. It's just like Keela's."

"Red hair is a colour we don't have in our family," Damien commented. "Mine and the twin's hair are the only different ones out of all of us. Everyone else has dark brown hair."

"Things are changing, little brother." Ryder chuckled. "You aren't the odd one out anymore."

Damien snorted as he gazed at the picture of his nephew. "He looks like Jax."

"He does," I agreed. "And that means he looks like Locke because those two are the double of Kane, and Nixon and Jules look just like you, Ry. There are so many mini Slater lads."

"Then there is Georgie who is a Murphy girl to the core." Damien chuckled.

"She has Nico's dimples, so she's not *entirely* a Murphy. She has some Slater genes in 'er. Don't worry about that."

After two more hours of waiting, the lads were finally ready to leave work, and we headed straight to the hospital. I practically sprinted ahead of them once I knew what floor and ward Keela and the baby were on.

"Are you crying'?" I called out to Alec, whose smile stretched from ear to ear as he came to greet us.

"No," he called back, wiping under his eyes. "It's liquid pride."

I had to get a running start, but I surprised myself and possibly everyone else when I quite literally jumped into Alec's arms. He laughed as I wrapped my legs around his waist and encircled my arms tightly around his neck. He returned my hug just as tight, and he vibrated with joyous laughter.

"You're a daddy!" I squealed and pulled back to look at him.

I had said that exact thing to Ryder when the twins were born, and his smile was identical to Alec's.

"I'm a daddy." He smiled, and when I kissed his cheek and hugged him again, he laughed harder.

"How badly do you want to punch me, little brother?"

"Because your kid was just born, I'm going to go easy on you and stick with a solid six."

"That's a weak score, considering your girl is *wrapped* around me."

"If you move your hands from her thighs to her ass," Damien growled, "then you'll die right here."

"You mean if I move them to where I can feel *everything* … I'm joking!"

Alec quickly set me down to appease Damien, and he looked so happy that his smile was infectious.

"I think my baby brother is possessive of you, Lana."

When an arm was slung over my shoulder, and I was tugged against a hard body, I snorted.

"That's not news to me, daddy-o."

"Okay," Damien grunted. "That's enough of you calling him that."

"What?" I questioned as I looked up at him. "Daddy?"

"Yeah," Damien replied. "The only person you call daddy is *me*."

I felt my face flame, and when Damien laughed, so did his brothers.

"I don't call 'im that," I said, glancing around. "I don't."

"You have called me it plenty—"

"*You* need to shut your bloody mouth," I cut Damien off with a squeak.

He had a shit-eating grin on his face but did as asked.

"What did ye' call the baby?"

Alec dimpled. "Go ask Keela."

"I'll do just that," I chirped. "This kid is the sixth cousin, and the seventh is comin' along soon if Bronagh has anythin' to say about it. You baby-makin' machines are goin' to have me broke with birthdays and Christmas!"

I chose that moment to dart down the corridor, leaving the brothers chuckling behind me.

"Oh, Keela," I whispered as I saw my first visual of her sitting in her hospital bed with a tiny bundle in her arms.

She looked up at me, and though she was clearly exhausted, I had never seen her look more beautiful.

"Come meet Enzo Brandon Slater."

I squealed as I covered my mouth with my hands and inched closer. Enzo's mop of bright red hair was the first thing to gain my full attention.

"He has so much hair like the twins when they were born," I whispered. "I love 'im already."

When Keela carefully handed him to me, I sat down on the large chair next to her bed, and I stared down at Enzo in complete awe.

"Where did ye' get his first name from?"

"*Vampire Diaries*," Keela answered with a snort. "I loved the name when I heard it years ago; I'm still surprised Alec liked it. Brandon is after me uncle, of course. He's pulled his fair share of shite when it came to me and Alec, but he's always been there for me, no matter what. He's been really good to Alec too since we've put the past behind us."

I traced my fingertip over Enzo's button nose. The action disturbed him, and he silently opened his eyes and stared up at me. I knew I was most likely a blurry picture to him, but I felt like he could see me.

"Hi, Enzo." I smiled. "I'm your Auntie Alannah."

He made a little coo sound, then yawned. The action was so small, so insignificant, yet I felt it all the way down to my soul. I wanted this. I wanted a baby. Damien's baby.

"Oh God," I whispered.

"What?" Alec asked.

I hadn't realised he had entered the room.

"I think I'm feelin' broody."

Silence, then Alec snickered. "Fifty euros she's pregnant by next week."

Chuckles sounded, and when I looked up, my eyes instantly locked on Damien's. He was smiling and staring at me with so much love and admiration that it caused my heart to pound hard against my chest.

"I want one."

His smile vanished, and his lips parted ever so slightly.

"*This* one?" he eventually asked. "I don't think my brother would agree to that."

Alec snorted as he came to Keela's side and sat on her bed with her, putting his arm around her shoulder.

"I'll settle for one who looks like 'im," I mused. "Slater genes are strong. I think ye'll give me a handsome little man like this … minus the red hair."

Damien stared at me. "Are you teasing?"

"No," I answered. "I want a baby."

Kane looked at Damien, then at me and said, "I think he is in shock, Alannah."

"I think you're right, Kane. I don't think he believes me," I mused. "I think I'll have to show 'im how serious I am."

Keela sat up. "You can't have sex in a maternity hospital, Alannah. Vaginas are meant to be sore 'ere, not throbbin' for sex."

When I chuckled, it disturbed Enzo, who was still looking up at me.

"He is *really* staring at you," Alec commented when he leaned a little closer. "I think you're his first crush, Lana."

I snorted, then playfully rolled my eyes when the rest of the lads wholeheartedly agreed.

"Do ye' think his eyes will change colour or stay dark blue like this?"

"I think they'll be grey like Alec's," Keela commented. "All the boys had dark blue eyes when they were born, but they're all grey now. Georgie is the only one who has green eyes, but that's because she's a carbon copy of Bronagh."

I agreed.

I looked at my friend. "How sore was it?"

"*Sore*," Keela grunted. "Jesus, I thought I was goin' to die, then when he was born, it all went away. It's weird, but I can't even remember what it felt like, and I only had 'im a little while ago."

I looked down at Enzo.

"I figured if Bronagh can do it, so can I."

Keela laughed, then winced. Alec was practically in her face asking what was wrong.

"Nothin'," she assured him. "I'm sore and laughin' hurt a little. It's no biggie."

Alec looked at me. "Don't make her laugh again."

Keela laughed at how serious he was, then winced once more. Alec cringed and appeared angry with himself for making her laugh. I looked back down at Enzo, who had finally drifted back into a comfortable sleep. I handed him over to Ryder when he moved forward.

"This is weird," he commented. "I think that my twins are small, but holding this little man just shows how big they've gotten."

"Your lads are one in six months," I reminded him.

"Don't talk about that," he groaned. "It freaks me out."

I chuckled as I got to my feet and walked towards Damien whose attention was solely on me.

"What's that look for?"

"Were you serious?" he asked. "About wanting a baby?"

"As serious as a heart attack."

Damien frowned. "Alannah, this is what we've been arguin' about. You said you wanted to wait until you were ready for marriage and a baby."

That was two days ago.

"I spoke to Bronagh about it, and I realised somethin'."

"What?"

"That there is never goin' to be a perfect time to have a baby and get married. I'm *always* goin' to be busy with work, God willin', and you're goin' to be flat out over the next few years with your apprenticeship. I'm not goin' to pretend that I'm not scared at how fast things are movin' for us, but I'm goin' to learn to take things one day at the time with you. Things are simpler that way."

Damien licked his lower lip. "Does that mean you want to marry me?"

"Yeah, it does, so when you want to propose to me again, be prepared for *that* answer."

CHAPTER EIGHT

Damien hadn't proposed to me … yet.

It confused me but didn't upset me because I knew men had a lot of mental preparation to go through when they were popping the question … especially when the last three times Damien asked, the answer was no. The day after Keela gave birth to Enzo, she came home, and we all showed up at her and Alec's house to fawn over the baby and congratulate our friends.

Bronagh managed five minutes before she started crying, but she had no idea why, and the woman was tearing Nico up from how distraught he appeared to be. She asked me to go to the supermarket with her, so she could walk around and hopefully put herself into labour. Nico was visibly terrified, but I assured him that I would take care of her.

"Why are you so keen on givin' the man a heart attack?"

"I don't mean to worry 'im, but he is no help when I'm restless. I feel like I can't breathe when I'm inside."

I understood.

"Are ye' uncomfortable?"

"Unbelievably," she grunted as she adjusted her seat belt. "I'm sore, tired, cranky, and just *so* fuckin' ready for this baby to come. It's not fair that Keela was so small and not bothered about bein' pregnant longer than 'er due date. I hate 'er."

I laughed as I adjusted the driver's seat in Nico's car. "No, you don't."

"No." Bronagh sniffled. "I don't. I love 'er and 'er perfect little boy."

She was breaking my heart.

"We'll get that kid out of you today if it's the last thing we do, okay?"

Bronagh bobbed her head. "Okay."

I drove to our local Tesco that was only five minutes away, and though we just wanted to walk around, Bronagh decided to get some messages while she was there. If she *did* go into labour, then by the time she got home with her new baby, at least her house would be stocked with food. That was how we looked at it. I got a trolley, then gave it to Bronagh to push, just so she would have something to lean on. Her feet were swollen, so anything to take some pressure off them was a must.

"Where to first?"

"Just keep walkin' straight, then we'll walk up and down each aisle," Bronagh answered. "There's an unspoken rule about things bein' one way in this shop. Anyone who walks the wrong way will just have to wait until I walk by to get around me because I'm not movin' for anyone."

"Okay, mama bear," I appeased. "Your way or the motorway."

Bronagh chuckled tiredly. She then pointed out what items she wanted me to pick up and put into the trolley as we approached them. We did this for thirty minutes. I answered ten calls from Nico during that time. The poor man would need to be sedated once this child was born because his nerves were *fried*. We had just come to the cereal aisle when I noticed an overweight, middle-aged man leering at Bronagh.

An uncomfortable chill ran up my spine, and my protective instinct kicked in. I moved over and stood directly in front of her, blocking her as much as I could. When I glanced at the man once more, his roaming eyes were now on me, and it didn't take a genius to guess what disgusting thoughts were running through his mind.

"Let's go."

"Wait," Bronagh said. "What's nicer, Cornflakes or Special K?"

"Just get both."

My friend frowned. "What's wrong?"

"The man behind us," I mumbled. "He is lookin' at us in a way that's makin' me skin crawl."

To her credit, Bronagh tried to be discreet as she glanced his way, but when she caught sight of him and saw for herself how he was ogling us, her face dropped.

"He's creepy."

I agreed.

"Let's just go," I mumbled. "I don't like how he is lookin' at us."

She tossed both boxes of cereal into the trolley, and together, we walked away. When we reached the till and glanced back over our shoulders, we both released a sigh of relief when we saw that the man hadn't followed us. Logically, I knew he was most likely harmless, but I couldn't shake the feeling of unease that settled over me when I realised that he was watching us.

After we checked out all our items, we put them into carrier bags, popped them into the trolley, and left the shop. We had just cleared the exit and turned the corner only to have the creepy man step in front of our trolley and cause us to come to an abrupt halt. I grabbed Bronagh's forearm and held on.

"Excuse us," I said. "We'd like to get by, please."

"You're both real pretty," he said, and when he spoke, I could see how yellow his teeth were. "Real pretty."

"Thank y-you," I stammered. "But we *have* to go."

I tried to turn the trolley to move around the man, but he stepped back in front of us. That was the moment I knew this was a bad situation, and it wasn't going to have a good outcome.

"I have a husband," Bronagh blurted the lie with ease. "And so does she."

The man looked between us.

"You both *really* playin' the married card?"

"We *are* married," Bronagh pressed. "I'm pregnant with me second child, as if you can't see that for yourself."

The man didn't move a muscle.

"Pregnant women fetch a high price on the streets."

Excuse me?

"Please, leave us alone," I asked him, my voice soft. "We're just 'ere to do some shoppin'."

"I can offer ye' both jobs," he spoke, ignoring me completely. "I can make ye' both wealthy women. All ye' have to do is join me entertainment business."

Entertainment business?

"We don't want to work for ye'," I said, my voice firm. "We aren't—"

"You have a big mouth." The man cut me off. "I bet you can deep throat. That earns me worker's big tips."

"Workers?" Bronagh repeated. "What are you talkin' about?"

"Women of the night." The man grinned. "Or day. Whenever you get a body between your thighs, really."

"Prostitution?" I choked. "We are *not* gonna be prostitutes!"

What the fuck kind of conversation is this?

"Don't raise your voice at me," the man snapped.

Bronagh pushed the trolley forward, and it smacked the man's thigh and sent him stumbling back.

"Clear off!" she warned. "We don't want no part of your business."

"You'll fuckin' pay for that!"

When he turned and stormed away, my heart was pounding erratically.

"We have to leave!" I stressed to Bronagh. "I feel sick."

"Me too," Bronagh agreed.

Together, we hustled across the car park, only to come to an abrupt halt when we saw a black-haired woman and a red-haired woman jogging towards us with the fat man huffing and puffing as he trailed behind them.

"Oh God."

I scrambled for my phone, and when I rooted it out of my bag, I called Nico straight away. He answered on the second ring.

"Nico?"

"Alannah?" he said. "What's up?"

"We need help," I said, my voice gruff. "A man was bein' creepy towards us in the shop so we told 'im off, and now we're in the car park and he is 'ere with two women who I think are goin' to fight us. I'm afraid I won't be able to protect Bronagh. She can't get to the car without them gettin' 'er first."

Nico wasted zero time as he asked which part of the car park we were in. When I hung up the phone, the women and the man were only metres away from us.

"Alannah," Bronagh said, her grip tightening on me. "I think they're goin' to jump me. Look at them."

I eyed the two girls and noticed they were removing earrings, repositioning rings on their fingers, and tying their hair back into tight buns. It didn't look good, and I suddenly felt sick because I was going to get hurt by one or both of these women. No way in hell was I standing by while they jumped my friend.

"She is pregnant," I announced, loudly. "Don't even *think* of comin' for 'er."

Both the women laughed, uncaringly.

"I'm not jokin'," I pressed. "We did nothin' wrong."

"You hit me baby's daddy with your trolley!" the redhead spat. "I'm gonna bounce your head off the concrete."

Christ.

"She has a baby with 'im?" Bronagh said under her breath. "She's half his age and *way* out of his league."

I stared at the women, then said, "I think they work for 'im, and he mixed business with pleasure."

"Oh."

Yeah, oh.

"He cornered us and tried to get us to work for 'im," Bronagh said in our defence. "He wouldn't go away when we asked 'im to."

"Ugly bitch!"

"Hey!" I snapped, shocked that the man would insult my friend. "You can't just slag 'er off because she wouldn't work as your prostitute! Ye' can't be serious to think ye' can just come out and ask strangers this kind of stuff!"

The women picked that moment to advance, and even though I was terrified, I quickly walked towards them just to keep them as far away from Bronagh as possible. I heard Bronagh's scream before I felt the first punch to the side of my head. I was knocked around like a ragdoll as both women punched, kicked, and stomped on me without mercy. I didn't even realise I was on the ground until I felt the concrete scrape my bare shoulders.

A fighter I was not, but I swung my closed fists and smacked one of the women hard enough to make her cry out. I managed to get to my feet and pushed both women away from me. One tumbled to the ground, but the other remained standing. My face was throbbing, my scalp stung, and the metallic taste of blood filling my mouth told me I was hurt. I spat it out and forced myself to relax when I saw everything I spat was blood and not saliva, and my mouth was filling up once more.

"You're bleedin'!" Bronagh whimpered, then I felt her hands clutch my waist. "Oh, shite. Alannah!"

I kept my focus on the two women; the one with red hair had her hand over her eye, and the one with black hair held her stomach. I wasn't sure if I really hurt them or not, but they didn't seem all that interested in running at me again, and I hoped to God they wouldn't. My nerves were shot, and I trembled as adrenaline shot through me. I turned my head when screeching tyres sounded, and I heard, "Alannah!"

Bronagh practically deflated with relief behind me.

"Dominic!"

I glanced to my left, and my heart pounded when I saw the twins running towards us. I had never been more relieved in my entire life to see the lads, and when they reached us, I had to spit again because my mouth was full of blood once more.

"Fuck!" Damien snapped as he grabbed my face and inspected it. "Who hurt you?"

"Those women," I answered, then quickly wiped my chin when spit spilled from it. "I can't *believe* this is happenin'."

When I looked at my hand, it was red with blood, and I knew something was wrong inside my mouth. Damien told me to open my mouth, so I did, and when he stuck a finger inside and felt along the inside of my cheek, he ran his finger over a part of flesh that made me jerk away in pain.

"There's a gash on the inside of your cheek," he said, his jaw tensed. "How did that happen?"

"It must have been when one of them punched or kicked me head," I answered, not knowing how else it could have happened. "Maybe one of me teeth cut it?"

Nico looked me over once he made sure Bronagh was okay, and when I had to spit again, he saw the blood on the ground, on my hands, and running down my chin. He looked as furious as Damien. He asked me to show him my mouth and used the torch on his phone so he could have a better look.

"It's a bad cut," he concluded. "I think you'll need stitches."

I sucked in a sharp breath, and Damien instantly got in my space.

"Look at me," he said and wouldn't speak until I locked eyes on him. "It's fine. We'll go to the hospital and get you all fixed up."

I opened my mouth to speak, but when I had to spit again, I began to believe that Nico was right. At that moment, my face began to throb with pain, and like I knew I eventually would, I began to cry. To avoid having the women who attacked me see my breakdown, I pressed my face against Damien's chest and tried my best to hold it in, but once the first whimper came, it paved the way for the sobs.

"Oh, Lana," Bronagh said as she placed her hand above Damien's hands on my back. "Are you okay?"

I could only nod to reassure her, but I was scared, and crying was the only way I could relieve my stress when I had no paint or my sketching pad on hand. I hated that when I cried, I couldn't talk without hiccupping or a sob breaking my sentence. Damien hugged my body to his and wordlessly swayed me side to side. When I had to pull back and spit on the ground again, he looked over his shoulder and snapped, "Don't either of you three fucking move!"

When I had calmed down a bit, Damien turned to face the trio, and he was enraged.

"Who the fuck do you think you are?" he bellowed.

"It was a misunderstandin'," the creepy man stated. "I swear."

"Liar!" I snapped. "Ye' insinuated we should work as your prostitutes, and when we cleared you off, ye' got those women to attack me! What in God's name is the matter with ye'?"

I jumped back when Damien rapidly closed the gap between him and the man, getting in his space.

"I fucking *know* you didn't insult my sister-in-law *and* threaten her and my girl, you fat fuck."

The man seemed to size Damien up, and he concluded what I did. While he was a few inches shorter than Damien, the man was stockier. It all happened fast. My scream died in my throat when the man suddenly swung his fist, but Damien bobbed his head to the left like he expected it. The man caught nothing but air while Damien slammed his fist into the man's gut, causing the man to hunch forward with a wheeze. I squealed when Damien rammed his knee into the man's face. Blood instantly spurted from the man's nose. He yelled in pain and used both his hands to cover his injury.

My heart pounded against my chest so fast I thought it would explode.

Damien threw a single jab, but the sound of it connecting was like a slap of wet skin. I cringed just as the man dropped to one knee. He shook his head, put his hand on his jaw, then fell onto his behind.

He looked completely dazed and made no attempt to get back up, so Damien didn't bother to hit him again since he now posed no threat. Instead, he focused on the two women who were screeching like banshees. The redhead attempted to dash at Bronagh, but Nico surged forward, putting himself in front of Bronagh and completely blocking her from the girl's view and range.

"If you put your hands on my wife," he snarled at the women, "I'm putting *my* hands on *you*."

Oh, fuck.

The redhead glanced at the dazed man on the ground, then she wisely abandoned attacking Bronagh and moved to help him. The black-haired woman didn't aid her. Her burning gaze turned on me, and she took a dangerous step towards me, but my view was suddenly blocked when Damien moved in front of me. My hands automatically went to his waist, and I gripped him tightly.

"Try it," he warned the woman, his voice dangerously low. "I fucking *dare* you."

"What'll ye' do?" she sneered. "Ye' gonna hit me too?"

"I will do anything necessary to keep your hands off her," he countered. "I don't give a *fuck* if you're a woman. If you lay a hand on my girl, I'm treating you like a man."

My lips parted, and I prayed the woman wouldn't be foolish enough to test Damien, not when he sounded so furious. I heard the woman curse at Damien, and when I peeked around him, I saw she was now helping the redhead get the injured man to his feet. The three of them walked away slowly, but they did so with jeers and insults thrown our way. Bronagh was called fat, and I was called ugly.

"I'm pregnant, dopey hole, not fat!"

"Yeah," I shouted, "and I'm not ugly!"

When Bronagh and I looked at one another, for some reason, we started to laugh. The situation wasn't funny at all, not in the slightest, but we laughed anyway. That was until I whimpered in pain and spat blood, again. Damien turned, gripped my arm, and wordlessly steered me towards Alec's Sportage that the twins obviously borrowed to come to our rescue. I climbed into the back seat with him, and Nico and Bronagh climbed into the front.

"The messages!" I shouted. "They're in the trolley."

The twins hurriedly got the bags of food and put them in the boot of the car.

"Nico, your car is parked—"

"I'll come back for it later, we need to get you to the hospital."

I nodded, mutely.

"I can't believe that just happened!" Bronagh stated, and she buckled her seat belt. "All because we told that creep that we weren't interested in workin' for 'im. Fuckin' ridiculous."

I grunted. "Can you *believe* he asked us to come and work for 'im as prostitutes? He was dead bloody serious when he asked us that, Bronagh."

"I know!" she said, amazed. "He even promised to make us wealthy women from it."

We were silent for a moment, then we laughed again. I only stopped when I felt how rigid Damien was. I looked at him and found his gaze was locked out the window, and his hands balled into fists. He was still mad; there was no getting around that. I wanted to ask him if he was okay, but I had to spit, so I grabbed an empty fast food restaurant cup from the cup-holder next to me and spat into it. Damien looked at me, then at the cup, and then at my face.

"Put your tongue against the wound," he said. "It might help with the bleeding."

I attempted it but screeched when a burning hot pain filled my cheek.

"Hurts," was all I could say.

Damien reached over and grabbed my hand. He didn't seem to care that I still had blood on my skin; he squeezed my hand reassuringly, and I was pleased to find that it helped me relax massively. I spat into the cup again a few minutes later and began to sniffle as the pain became bad. Under my eyes throbbed, my scalp felt like it was on fire, and my cheek stung like hell. I knew, at that moment, that I would never be able to make it as an underground fighter like Nico once was. My pain tolerance was zero.

"We're nearly there, Alannah," Nico said softly when my cries could be heard.

Bronagh reached her hand back and touched my knee, the gesture comforting me.

"I can't believe this happened."

"Thanks, Alannah," Bronagh said in response.

"For what?"

"Defendin' me," she answered. "Babe, they were goin' to hurt me, and you threw yourself at them so they wouldn't."

I blinked. "You're me best friend."

"I know, and I love ye'."

"I love ye' too."

Silence lingered for a moment until I said, "If that situation didn't scare that baby out of you, then I'm afraid nothin' will."

Bronagh laughed. I squeezed my eyes shut and tried to block out all the pain that seemed to hit me at once. I focused on Damien.

"How are you here?"

"Dominic pulled up at the shop, told me what was going on, and I jumped in Alec's car."

My heart squeezed.

"This really hurts."

"I know, baby."

We arrived at the hospital ten minutes later, and as soon as we entered the A&E Department and checked in, I was taken straight to the back and put inside a cubicle. Damien accompanied me while Nico and Bronagh had to wait outside. I was given a cardboard bedpan and told to spit into that whenever I had to. Damien grabbed plenty of tissues and dabbed at my mouth whenever blood dribbled out of my mouth before I could spit.

"Me eye feels bleedin' huge."

"It's swelling," Damien said through gritted teeth.

I stared up at him. "Are ye' mad at me?"

"No," he answered. "Just mad that this happened to you."

He moved closer to me and put his arms around my body. I pressed my face gently against him and waited. We stayed like that for at least twenty minutes. Damien didn't move away from me; he remained standing and held me to him. He held the bedpan under my mouth so I could spit when I had to. When a doctor came and saw the bedpan, he asked Damien to step aside so he could examine me. He asked me to lie back on the bed and open my mouth, and when I did, tears instantly fell from my eyes with the pain.

"You've got yourself a sore one."

He didn't have to tell me twice.

"You'll have to have stitches."

I tried to get up, but Damien held me in place, so I began to cry harder.

"Stop," he said and placed a kiss on my shoulder. "I don't want to hurt you, freckles. Stop."

I couldn't help it. My fight or flight reaction kicked in, and I wanted to run away.

"We'll sedate you," the doctor assured me. "You won't feel a thing."

"Sedation?" Damien repeated. "It's a cut on her cheek. Why does she need to be sedated?"

"The angle of it is difficult to stitch while she is awake," the doctor explained. "If I tug and move the needle around while she is conscious, it will hurt her greatly, and she would undoubtedly move and most likely injure herself further. This will take me ten minutes to do with her asleep. She'll be snoozing, then stitched and awake all in half an hour this way."

Damien looked down at me. "You understand him?"

I nodded, but the movement caused me pain, so I stopped. A nurse came in and asked me a million questions then asked me to sign something to allow me to be sedated by an anaesthesiologist. Damien was so mad that I signed the form without reading it, but I didn't care. My face throbbed, and my head overall felt like a dead weight on my shoulders. I just wanted to go to sleep. Damien held my hand as a nurse stuck a needle in my arm and set up an IV.

I was moved to the operating theatre where I had to strip out of my clothes and put on a disposable gown. Once the nurses confirmed I had no food or water since early in the morning, they wheeled my bed into the operating room. Damien kissed me and told me he'd ring my parents as soon as he got back to Dominic and Bronagh who were still in the A&E Department. I was brave for him because I could see how worried he was for me, especially when the nurse had to clean up blood that dribbled from my mouth.

Once inside the operating room, things moved fast and before I knew it, I was asked to count back from ten. I think I made it to six before I was gifted with darkness. Sweet, painless darkness.

CHAPTER NINE

One week later...

"Y ou have a visitor."

I groaned and turned over, putting my back to Damien.

"I said *no* visitors," I grouched. "How stupid are ye' not to comprehend that?"

"I must be *very* stupid for putting up with your nasty attitude this past week."

I grunted. "No one asked ye' to put up with it."

"Wrong," he replied. "Your mom did because she said she was gonna slap you silly if you snapped at another person while you healed."

"I wouldn't snap at people if they didn't do stupid stuff."

"You made Alec cry when you yelled at him."

"He made *'imself* cry," I scowled. "Who thinks chocolates are a good gift to bring someone who can't fuckin' *eat* anythin'?"

"He had good intentions," Damien replied. "Now he won't come back here unless you give him a formal handwritten apology."

"He'll be waitin' until hell freezes over if that's the case."

Damien sighed, long and deep.

"I want a cup of tea, Damien," I stated. "I wouldn't be so

96

grouchy if ye' just gave me what I wanted."

"You can't have hot liquids until your stitches are fully dissolved and your wound is healed so *no tea.*"

"You're a real arsehole. I hope ye' know that. This is why I haven't had sex with ye' in a week."

"Jesus," a voice from the hallway sounded. "I'll just come back another time. She sounds like ... like the old *Bronagh.*"

I froze. "Is that Gavin Collins?"

"No," Gavin replied from the hallway. "It's not me."

Damien snorted. "It is him, and he came to see you, so get up."

"Or what?"

"Or I'll *make* you get up."

I didn't move, and when Damien moved and pulled my blanket away from my body, I sat up in a huff.

"I'm up," I snapped.

He rolled his eyes over me. "You need to shower."

"*You* need to piss off," I countered. "Me face is killin' me."

"Get up," he ordered. "I need to change the sheets."

I rolled my eyes as I put my face in my hands and groaned. I was an irritable monster, and I knew it, but every little thing Damien did annoyed me. Every little thing everyone did annoyed me. My friends and parents stopped coming to see me three days ago. My own mother refused to see me until I lost my attitude. A cup of tea would make me feel immensely better, but Damien refused me that. Seven long days it had been since I last had a cup of tea, and I was going through severe withdrawals. It was what fuelled my rude behaviour.

"I can't stand ye'," I said to Damien. "Not even a little bit."

He swatted my behind as I got up and passed him.

"I'm five seconds away from throwing you out of the damn window, *sweetheart.*"

"Ha! Ye' aren't strong enough to pick me up and throw me out the window ... Ye' aren't Nico."

I knew I would hit a nerve with that, and from the glare Damien shot my way, I knew he would get me back for it in some shape or form. I left the room, and when I saw Gavin in the hallway, I scowled.

"Hello to you too, Alannah."

I ignored him as I leaned my shoulder against the wall.

"Have ye' thrown water in another pregnant woman's face lately?"

"Yeah," I lied. "That's me thing. I prey on the weak and vulnerable."

Gavin snorted. "I miss ye'."

"Don't let the midget hear ye' say that," I grunted. "She'll skin *me* alive."

"Alannah." Gavin sighed. "Kalin doesn't hate—"

"Yeah," I cut him off. "She does. Anyone with eyes can see it; she hates that we're friends. She doesn't care that you're Bronagh's friend, just *mine*. I don't care, though. I don't need 'er to be me friend. She's a hobbit-sized demon."

I was blatantly ignoring the fact that we were the exact same height and so was Gavin.

"*I* need ye' to be her friend," he pressed. "I love ye', Alannah, and I want ye' to be around me son, but Kalin won't let that happen if ye' both keep … whatever feud ye' both have goin'."

"Feud?" I repeated, wide-eyed. "Gavin, she glares at me and gives me foul looks whenever me and you hug or talk to one another. How can ye' *not* see she has a problem with me? I would never, *never* treat a person like she treats me. I'm nice, and she is makin' me not nice, which goes against everythin' I am as a person! I'm even nice to Micah Daley when I see 'er, and she is the *devil*!"

Gavin's shoulders slumped, and I knew that he agreed with me.

"I'm convinced that she thinks we secretly like each other, which is *so* stupid because anyone with eyes can see how much I love that irritable arsehole in the bedroom."

"You're so sweet, baby."

"Bite me!"

"I will later."

I scowled as I refocused on a now amused Gavin.

"Look," he said, straightening up. "I'm goin' to 'er apartment to talk about this once and for all because I want you two to be friends *before* me kid is born."

I didn't move.

"I'll be 'ere if she wants to talk to me," I said. "I look like the back end of a dog, so I'm *not* leavin' this apartment."

Gavin frowned. "Bear, ye' don't—"

"Don't waste your breath," Damien called from the bedroom. "She'll insult you if you compliment her or be nice in *any way* possible. Trust me, buddy."

I glared over my shoulder but said nothing as I turned back to face Gavin, who was silently chuckling.

"I'll be back later."

I pushed away from the wall. "Don't be surprised if Kalin gives you hell over this."

Gavin left my apartment seeming very determined while I headed into the bathroom and took a long, hot shower. I was just about finished when I felt a cold breeze touch my skin before it was replaced with strong hands. I closed my eyes when Damien's naked body pressed against me, and his lips found their way to my neck. I felt how hard he was, but he didn't touch me in a way that showed he was in any hurry to take me, which surprised me. We hadn't had sex since I got hurt, and I didn't blame him for not touching me.

I had been a massive bitch.

"I'm sorry," I said, lowering my head. "I'm *so* sorry for bein' rude to you."

I felt Damien's nose rub against my neck.

"Everyone must think I'm a bitch," I continued before I lifted my hands to my face. "I feel horrible."

"Baby," Damien said, his voice gruff. "Everyone knows you were physically hurting, and that it messed with your mood. We all know you aren't a mean person, trust me."

I leaned my head back against his chest. I was physically hurting, but it was my nightmares that had me sleep deprived. They hadn't gone away. I closed my eyes, and tears fell before I could stop them. I sniffled, and Damien sighed as he turned me to face him.

"Don't cry, freckles," he said. "No one is mad at you."

"It's not that," I said, swallowing.

Damien pushed my wet hair out of my face.

"Then what is it?"

I stared up at him. "I don't want to worry ye'."

He tensed. "Tell me. Now."

I had to tell him. Keeping my thoughts to myself was eating me up inside.

"I'm havin' nightmares," I whispered. "About Morgan."

Damien's eyes widened ever so slightly. He didn't say a word as he reached over my shoulder, turned off the shower, and hustled us out of it. He wrapped a towel around his hips and grabbed a large one to wrap around me. He led me out of the room and into our bedroom. We both sat on the end of our bed and stared at each other.

"How long?"

I didn't play dumb. "The last few weeks," I answered.

"Why didn't you tell me?" he asked, and I heard the hurt in his voice.

"Because." I wiped under my nose. "I didn't want to worry ye'."

"Alannah," Damien scowled. "We're a couple ... partners. We deal with issues *together*, never apart."

I bobbed my head. "I know, and I'm so sorry. I just ... I didn't want ye' to think about 'im."

"I *always* think about him, about my past, but that shouldn't stop you from *talking* to me."

"I'm sorry," I repeated. "I thought I was doin' the right thing, but I wasn't. These nightmares are killin' me."

"Tell me about them."

I exhaled a deep breath.

"He always has you and your brothers tied up, and either hurts you badly or kills ye', but lately ..."

"Lately what?"

"Lately, he's been slittin' me throat, and that is when I wake up."

Damien looked a mixture of furious and terrified.

"He always tells me that he is in me head, which is what he planned all along. He tells me I don't really love ye' or want a marriage and a family with you because ye' could die and leave me, our kids could die and leave me. He says a lot of horrible things."

Damien frowned. "Is ... is that why you keep saying no when I propose?"

My shoulders slumped.

"Maybe. When I think about our future, I am absolutely terrified of you not bein' in it, so maybe Morgan is affectin' me. The bastard really did get into me head, just like he said he would."

Damien reached out and pulled me onto his lap.

"We've talked about this," he said. "You can't fear the future. None of us know what will happen."

"I know." I nodded. "I just love ye' so much that—"

"Baby, I know you love me," Damien cut me off. "And now I know why you've been so resistant and scared whenever we talk about our future. You want our future. You're just scared of it being anything less than perfect."

"Yes," I whispered.

He kissed the side of my head. "Morgan ... *Carter* is gone. I know I've struggled with him for a long time since he was here, but I'm not going to worry about him anymore, okay? I'm leaving him in my past just like he is leaving me in his."

My heart swelled. "Damien, I want that too."

"Look at me."

I did.

"We're *both* leaving him in our past," he said, firmly. "He has no power over us. He is nothing. Do you hear me? *Nothing.*"

"Nothin'," I repeated. "Morgan is nothin'."

When I spoke the words and felt Damien wrap me in his embrace, I felt lighter than I had in a long time. I realised what was happening. I was letting Morgan go and leaving everything to do with him in my past. In *our* past. I was free of him, and he would *never* mess with my head ever again. I wrapped my arms around Damien and squeezed him tightly. When I pressed my face into his shoulder, I forgot about my bruises and winced. When I pulled back, Damien leaned in and placed a kiss under my eye.

"Does it still look ugly?"

"So ugly." He nodded with a grin on his face. "It's such a chore to date you, the ugliest woman in the whole world."

When I laughed, I saw Damien's eyes light up.

"I love your laugh," he said. "It's such a happy sound, baby."

I rested my forehead against his. "*You* make me so happy."

"I know," he mused. "I'm perfect."

When I laughed again, he leaned us back onto the bed, rolled me under him, and spent the next hour loving my body until I thought my soul might leave it. When we finally left our bed, we both got dressed, and I dried the remaining damp sections of my hair before tying it up into a bun on top of my head. I put on my work clothes, kissed Damien long and hard—or as hard as my healing mouth would allow—then went into my studio. Damien started calling it a studio instead of an office as of late, and I've adapted it. Saying office reminded me of when *he* worked with me, and since I was leaving him in my past, I left my office there too.

"When the doorbell rang an hour later, I shouted, "Dame, can ye' get that?"

"Sure."

If it was Dante stopping by to annoy Damien, I was going to kill him.

"Baby, it's Gavin and Kalin."

I paused. I had completely forgotten about Gavin. I turned when Kalin entered my studio, and I wanted to snort when Damien and

Gavin hovered by the door as if we were just going to attack each other.

"The pair of you go play the Xbox or somethin'," I said. "Me and Kalin need to speak alone."

They didn't need to be told twice, so Damien closed the door and left us in peace. It was eerily silent for at least thirty seconds. Kalin stared at me, and I stared right back at her.

"What is your problem?"

She didn't answer.

"You're tapped in the head if you think Gavin is gonna cut me from his life just because *you* don't like me. We're best friends, do ye' understand that? I love 'im, and he loves me. We're like brother and sister, and not *you* or the fact that you're the mother of his child can change that. Ever."

Kalin folded her arms across the top of her bump, but still, she said nothing.

"Well?" I demanded. "What do you have to say for yourself?"

"I'm sorry."

"I don't give a ... what?"

"Ye' heard me," Kalin said, her head held high. "I said I'm sorry."

"Sorry for what?"

"Treatin' you the way I have been," she answered. "I've been jealous, very jealous of the relationship that ye' have with Gavin."

I *knew* it.

"I don't understand *why*, Kalin," I said with a sigh. "It's not romantic. It's never been like that with me and Gav. We really *are* just best friends."

"I know that *now*," she said. "Gavin spoke to me about the pair of ye' when he stopped by a while ago. *He really* spoke to me."

I tilted my head to the side. "D'ye like Gavin?"

"A lot." She nodded. "But he isn't interested in a relationship with me. Not when we first got together and not now."

I heard the hurt in her voice, and I frowned.

"I'm sorry."

"Don't be," she said. "I can't force 'im to want to be with me. He made it very clear that he doesn't want a girlfriend; it's why we've agreed to raise the baby together platonically."

I blinked. "Platonically? But last week Ryder said … well, he assumed."

"Oh, I *know* what he assumed." Kalin chuckled. "I wasn't feelin' well that day, and Gavin pretended to be sick 'imself to get the day off work. I thought it'd be funny to moan in the background. Dante and Harley showed up, bashed 'im, then made 'im go back to work with them."

I snorted. "Sounds like them."

Kalin glanced around the room. "You're crazy talented."

"Thanks," I said, then perked up. "I actually have somethin' for ye'."

"For *me*?"

I walked over to my canvas rack and plucked out the one on the bottom shelf.

"I painted this the day after your baby shower," I said and turned to face Kalin, holding up the canvas for her to see. "We had our fight, and ye' were on me mind, so I painted ye'."

Kalin's eyes instantly glazed over as she stepped closer.

"Alannah," she whispered. "It's beautiful. How did ye' do that?"

"It's what I do." I shrugged. "I figured it'd be a nice memento for you to have. I've done one for all of me friends during their pregnancies at some point."

Kalin looked up at me. "*Am* I one of your friends?"

"Yes." I nodded. "I think this conversation is us puttin' the rubbish behind us and focusin' on the future. We'd both be a lot happier, not to mention Gavin will be thrilled."

When Kalin laughed, her hands went to her belly and so did my eyes.

"Is he movin'?"

"Yeah." She smiled. "He is very active when he hears people's voices. It's like he wants to get his own say in."

"Can I ... can I feel 'im?"

"Of course."

I put the canvas down and placed my hands on Kalin's firm stomach, and instantly, I felt it move beneath me.

"Oh God," I said. "That's horrible."

Kalin laughed. "It feels weird, right?"

"Like an alien is tryin' to break free."

Kalin cracked up with laughter, and seconds later, the door of the room burst open and in fell Gavin and Damien. Damien looked at us, grunted, then shoved Gavin. "I *told* you she wouldn't hit a pregnant woman!"

"*You* thought it sounded like they were fightin' too." Gavin shoved him back.

They focused on us and what we were doing and relaxed.

"Does this mean what I think it means?"

"Yeah," I answered Gavin. "I'm leavin' Damien for Kalin. I'm a lesbian now."

Damien snorted, Gavin grinned, and Kalin giggled before she reached down and picked up the canvas I painted.

"Gav, look what Alannah did."

"Bear," he said, softly. "I love it."

Kalin's cheeks warmed, and my smile grew.

"Thanks. She looks great in it, huh?"

"Perfect," Gavin agreed, his eyes on the actual Kalin and not her painting.

I looked at Kalin, who was looking at the painting as her face burned, but she was obviously pleased with Gavin's response to it. We went into the kitchen, and while everyone else had tea, I had room temperature water.

"I feel like a junkie who needs a hit."

Gavin snorted. "This is the longest you've ever gone without tea."

"She's been a damn nightmare because of it."

"I really have been." I frowned. "I made Alec cry."

"I thought you said he made *himself* cry."

I scowled at Damien. "I was mean to 'im ... but he really was stupid bringin' me chocolates when I can't eat solid food."

Damien chuckled as I sat down on his lap. We talked to Gavin and Kalin for a while, and after they left, I decided to call Alec to apologise to him for how I behaved the last time I saw him. He answered on the fourth ring.

"Did you kill Damien in a fit of rage and decided to call me to confess it before you run away?"

"Yes," I answered. "Ye'll never find me. Damien is long gone ... just like your cup."

"You're an evil bitch," he quipped. "It hurts me whenever you bring my cup up, and you *know* it."

I laughed, and to Damien, I said, "He doesn't care that I killed ye', just that I mentioned his cup."

"I expect nothing less." Damien grinned as he settled onto the settee with his Xbox controller in hand.

"Do you still look like Quasimodo?"

I screeched. "*No!*"

Alec cracked up with laughter, and Damien looked at me with raised brows.

"He asked if I still looked like Quasimodo!"

Damien got that look someone gets on their face when they were trying desperately not to laugh.

"Laugh," I snarled to Damien. "I dare ye'."

"Leave my little brother alone, you bully."

I refocused on Alec. "How am *I* the bully?"

"Because you've been so mean this week. Damien said he was tempted to smother you in your sleep."

I couldn't help but snort. "He loves me too much to smother me."

Damien grinned as he played his game but clearly was listening to my conversation with his brother with one ear.

"Can we come over and see you?" Alec asked. "Keela is antsy to leave the house."

"Yeah, I wanna see the baby."

"*Just* the baby?"

"Yup," I answered. "I don't like *you* at all."

"Lies."

"Truths."

After we hung up, Damien and I lounged on the settee with Barbara as he played his video game. When the doorbell rang forty minutes later, I stood and left the room to answer it. When I opened the door, I blinked. Alec and Keela had brought the rest of our gang with them. Well, everyone bar Aideen and Ryder who were at work.

"You realise our apartment isn't as big as Kane and Aideen's, right?"

Everyone snorted as they filed into the apartment. Ever since we all made up six months ago, the gang made more of an effort to come around to my apartment to see me and Damien, just so we didn't have to be the ones travelling all the time. Jax and Georgie ended up in my arms, and winces were drawn from me when the kids poked at my fading bruises.

"Ah-ah," Bronagh chastised them. "Lana has a booboo."

"Booboo," Jax repeated then made a kissy noise.

When I walked into the sitting room, he leaned in and dramatically kissed my face.

"I swear he does that on purpose because he *knows* I can see him do it."

The men laughed while I rolled my eyes at Damien.

"Leave 'im alone. He is kissin' me booboo."

"*I'll* kiss your—"

"Shut *up!*"

"Both of you shut up." Bronagh grunted. "Nobody on planet Earth is as uncomfortable as me right now so be *quiet.*"

I sat down next to Damien, and Jax climbed over onto his lap where he gently petted Barbara who was curled up at Damien's side. That little traitor loved him way more than she loved me, and I was the feckin' one who rescued her. Damien handed Jax a console controller that wasn't switched on, so our nephew could 'play' the game on screen with his uncle.

"That's so cute," Branna said with a smile.

I looked at her and gazed at the twins who were both sleeping on her chest.

"How do they fall asleep so fast?"

"Ryder says they're like Damien," Branna answered. "Apparently, he can sleep on command."

"Tell me about it." I grunted. "His head touches the pillow, and he is out for the count."

Damien grinned but didn't comment.

"How come *you* aren't at work?" I asked Alec.

"Paternity leave."

I nodded, then said, "I'm sorry I made you cry."

He scowled. "I *didn't* cry. I told you all that dirt got in my eye and that was *it*."

"Sure," everyone said in unison and laughed.

"Either way," I continued, "I'm sorry for bein' a massive bitch to you all."

"You *were* pretty mean," Bronagh commented. "But considerin' ye' defended me when you were attacked for not wantin' to become a prostitute, who can blame ye'?"

"I *still* can't believe that happened!" Keela exclaimed. "Like, how does that happen in real life?"

"I don't know." I shivered. "But it was *horrible*."

Bronagh agreed with a bob of her head.

"How is your mouth?"

I looked at Kane and said, "Much better. I can still feel the stitches with me tongue, but they're dissolvin', slowly but surely."

"Have you had any tea yet?"

I shook my head to Branna's question and nodded towards Damien. "*He* won't let me."

"Jesus," Bronagh said. "No wonder ye' were like a witch. Ye've had no tea this entire week!"

"She can have it once her wound is fully closed." Damien sighed. "Another few days won't hurt. It'd be like putting salt on the wound if she drank it now with how much sugar she uses."

I piped down because that was the God's honest truth. I loved sugar in my tea.

"I have a question."

I looked at Alec.

"If you had to kiss one of the girls"—he grinned—"who would it be?"

I rolled my eyes. "You're a burden upon this world."

"Stop ruining my life and answer the damn question."

My lips twitched.

"Well, it'd have to be someone other than Bronagh since I already kissed 'er—"

"What?" Alec cut me off.

Kane leaned in closer. "What?"

Nico choked on air. "W-what?"

I laughed. "*What?*"

"You kissed Bronagh?"

I jumped after Damien whispered in my ear.

"Y-yeah," I stuttered, then cleared my throat. "Yeah, I did, but only when we were drunk forever ago because I thought me lips felt chapped, and she said they looked fine, and I said they *felt* chapped, so she kissed me and said it was all in me head because they felt soft to 'er so … yeah."

I was babbling, and I knew it, so I clamped my lips together to prevent myself from further embarrassment.

"How was it?"

I blinked. "What?"

"How was the kiss?"

I looked from Damien to Bronagh and back. "Fine."

"Better than fine," Bronagh corrected. "It was sexy."

It really wasn't, but I let her tease the lads.

"I wish I could have seen that."

"Me too," the brothers agreed with Alec

I focused on Nico.

"Someone else kissin' Bee turns you on?"

"No, no," Nico said. "The thought of another hot *female* kissing her turns me on. It's purely fantasy, though, because if it came down to the wire and Bronagh offered me a threesome with a woman, even a woman as hot as you, Lana, I'd say no. I want no woman other than my lady."

Even a woman as hot as me?

"Shut up, Nico."

I hated when he categorised me as hot because I knew he was just being polite because I was Bronagh's best friend. I was in no way ever fishing for compliments when I told him off for it either. I truly hated when he said it.

"What?"

Alec sighed. "She thinks you're full of it when you call her hot."

"You *are* hot, though," Nico concluded.

I scowled at him, and he winked in response.

"*I* think you're hot."

"I know *you* think I'm hot," I said to my better half. "Ye' can't keep your bloody hands off me."

Damien grinned. "I plan to keep my hands on you for a very long time, freckles."

Oh, I was counting on it.

CHAPTER TEN

Code red.

That was what I texted my best friend twenty minutes ago as I sat on the lid of my toilet and stared at the unopened box of tampons. They should have been opened and used by now but weren't. After Damien left for work, I followed my normal morning routine. I took care of Barbara, then got showered and changed into work clothes before I spent a few hours in my studio. When I took a break for lunch, I went into the toilet, and the second my eyes landed on my unopened box of tampons, my heart stopped.

I checked my personal calendar and determined my period was due exactly fourteen days ago, which was more than I originally thought. Normally, I wouldn't panic, but there were at least five of my birth control pills left in the package from last month, which told me I didn't take them on at least five days. Damien didn't use condoms when he had sex because I was on birth control. Birth control I wasn't taking correctly.

"Fuck," I whispered. "Fuck, fuck, *fuck*."

The front door to my apartment opened and closed.

"I'm 'ere!"

"Bathroom," I called out.

Bronagh barrelled into the room with a small pharmacy bag in her hand.

"I *never* thought you would text me code red." She panted. "You think you're *pregnant*?"

I nodded. "I'm two weeks late."

"Lana." She blinked. "Holy shite."

She quickly removed the contents of the bag, opened the pregnancy test box, and even though she had taken the tests before, she read the leaflet from top to bottom. She told me what to do and handed me a test. I wasn't shy as I lifted the lid of the toilet, pulled down my leggings and underwear, and peed on the stick. When I was finished, I capped the test, flushed the toilet, and washed my hands as I put it on the counter.

"You're shakin'," Bronagh commented.

I was. My entire body was.

"I'm scared."

"Don't be," Bronagh replied. "Ye' want this and so does Damien."

"But what if it ruins everythin'?" I asked, my heart pounding. "What if it's too much for Damien after everythin' we've gone through to become a couple? We're together five minutes, Bronagh."

She smiled warmly.

"Ye' *both* want this."

I inhaled and exhaled.

"I do ... We do. Jesus, I'm still terrified."

My friend laughed. "That never goes away, trust me."

I bobbed my knee up and down.

"How long do we have to wait?"

"A few more minutes."

I put my head in my hands. "Where's Georgie?"

"With Dominic," she answered. "He saw your text first, and he knows what code red means ... He said I told 'im ages ago."

I jerked my head up. "Bronagh."

"Relax," she said. "He isn't gonna phone Damien. He just said to phone 'im after Alannah talks to Damien so he knows if you're pregnant or not."

I nodded and put my head back in my hands.

"Ye' can check it now." Bronagh cleared her throat.

I couldn't move.

"Do it for me. Please."

I looked down as Bronagh lifted the test from the counter and peered down at it.

"What does it say, Bee?"

When she didn't respond, I looked up and found her smiling at me.

"Your eggo is preggo, mama."

I sucked in a sharp breath. "You're jokin'!"

Bronagh moved to my side and showed me the digital test.

Pregnant

2-3 weeks

"I'm pregnant," I whispered, then looked at Bronagh. "Bronagh, I'm gonna have a *baby!*"

She hugged me and promptly burst into tears. I didn't cry. I only hugged her and stared at myself through the mirror over her shoulder. I looked at the test again, just to make sure it wasn't faulty, then with Bronagh's encouragement, I took the other test that came in the box. It wasn't a digital test like the first one, but the two pink lines it revealed meant I was definitely pregnant.

"Fuck a duck," I said in amazement. "I think I'm in shock."

"*You're* in shock?" Bronagh repeated on a laugh. "Damien will *die!*"

My hands were shaking. "He wants this so bad."

"Then let's not make him wait," Bronagh squealed. "I'll have Dominic get 'im over to our house by the time we get there."

I nodded. "Do it."

When Bronagh and I entered her house, I could hear Nico and Damien laughing while Georgie squealed over something. I froze by the sitting room and couldn't make my feet move forward. Bronagh paused and looked at me.

"Tell 'im I want 'im," I said to my friend. "I have to tell 'im when it's just us."

Bronagh nodded and went into the kitchen while I entered the sitting room and stood there, looking down at my stomach.

"Alannah?"

I turned to face Damien and swallowed.

"What's wrong?"

My eyes welled up with tears.

Damien's eyes widened in alarm. "Is it your mom?"

I shook my head.

"Then what is it?"

I didn't answer.

"Alannah. Tell me."

I exhaled a breath. "I'm pregnant."

Damien stared down at me and said, "Shut up."

My heart stopped. "W-what?"

"You're lying," he said, his face the picture of disbelief. "You have to be."

"I'm not." I sniffled. "I took two tests. I have it here with me."

I rooted the tests out of my bag and handed them to him. He took them from me, brought them close to his face, and squinted his eyes before he rubbed them and stared at the tests once more.

"Alannah."

I know.

"You're having my baby?"

I couldn't speak, only nod.

He looked up at the ceiling and said, "Thank you, God."

When he looked back down at me, he kissed me without warning, then broke apart and pressed his forehead against mine.

"I can't believe this."

"Me either," I said. "I think I'm still in shock."

Damien placed his hands on either side of my face. "Are you happy?"

"Yes," I answered. "So happy ... just utterly terrified. Damien, we're havin' a baby."

"A baby," he repeated, and his lower lip wobbled. "We're having a *baby*, freckles."

Tears spilled over the brims of my eyes, and I laughed when he shouted, "I'm gonna be a daddy!"

I heard Nico and Bronagh cheer from the kitchen, and it only made us smile wider. Damien brought his hand to my stomach and flattened his palm over it, staring down at me with pure love and admiration.

"How far along do you think you are?"

"I've no idea," I answered. "Maybe four or five weeks, maybe less. The test says two to three weeks, but the package says that means four to five weeks pregnant. I missed me pill a few times, but I didn't even notice. I'm sorry."

"Sorry?" Damien repeated. "Baby, I'm on cloud nine right now."

"I know. I just don't want ye' to think I missed takin' the pills on purpose."

"I'm glad you didn't take them. You wouldn't be pregnant right now otherwise."

I smiled, then my jaw dropped just as Damien lowered to one knee.

"I'm glad you said no the first three times I asked you to marry me because I wasn't prepared if you had said yes," he said. "I wanted this time to be better, so that's why I've held off on asking you again. I wanted there to be candles, and a dinner I cooked for you, and romantic music, but I can't wait to ask you this when I know no other time would be sweeter than right now."

My heart skipped a beat.

"Damien."

He reached into his back pocket and pulled out a small black box. He opened the lid, and I sucked in a sharp breath when a small but beautiful diamond ring was revealed.

"I bought this the day after Enzo was born," he said, gazing up at me. "I've been working my ass off, taking all the hours and overtime I could get to buy this for you."

He took my left hand.

"The night your mom got the all clear in the hospital, I went to their house and asked them both for their permission to marry you. They gave me that permission and told me they loved me, Alannah. They called me son and accepted me into your family. Do you know how much that means to me? That they trust me with their only daughter?"

Tears spilled over the brims of my eyes.

"I know you're scared for the future, scared that I won't be in it, but you need to know that you aren't an option for me, Alannah. You're my priority. You and that baby you're carrying. I'm so in love with you, freckles. I've only ever wanted you, and if you let me, I want to scream to the world that I have you."

I felt like my heart was about to explode.

"Alannah Ryan." Damien licked his lips. "Will you marry me?"

"Yes," I breathed. "Yes, yes, *yes!*"

He removed the ring from the box and slid it onto my finger. It fit perfectly, and Damien sighed with relief before a huge smile overtook his face. He got to his feet and kissed me until I felt dizzy.

"I got all of that on video," Bronagh, who was in tears, announced from the doorway. "Good man yourself, Damien. I was about to accept your proposal if Alannah didn't."

Both Damien and I laughed as we hugged, kissed, and looked brightly to the future.

CHAPTER ELEVEN

Five days later...

"**O**h, my God!"
I dropped my phone with fright, then spun around and barrelled into the kitchen.

"What?" I shouted. "What's wrong?"

I scanned the room, looking for any signs of danger, and when I found nothing, I focused on Keela, who was staring at her phone with wide eyes. I looked to the left when I heard commotion, and I stepped forward when I saw Nico, Damien, and Ryder running down the hallway and all but falling into the kitchen.

"What is it?" Ryder demanded as he rushed over to Keela.

"There is an indie book signing in town next week, and I never bloody knew about it!"

A huge breath of relief left me.

"Bloody hell, Kay," I said and placed my hands on my hips. "You frightened the hell out of me."

"Us too," Damien grunted from behind me.

I loved how his voice surrounded me and made me feel all tingly and warm.

"I'm sorry, but this is serious," Keela stressed. "Oh. My. God. Indie royalty will be there, some of me *favourite* authors. I'm buying a ticket right now."

Her happiness was infectious.

"Get me one too, and I'll go with you. If you're this excited right now, I want to see how you'll be at the event."

The lads snorted from behind me.

Nico frowned at her. "Hasn't Alec talked to you about when you are screaming about books? You scream when one you want gets a release date, a summary thing, a cover, an excerpt thing, *and* when it releases. I told you it makes me think you're dying or something."

"I know, I'm sorry, but it's a *book signin'*, Nico," Keela said in awe. "Me people will be there."

I laughed. "*Your* people?"

Keela looked at me and nodded. "Book people. The best kind of people. They get me."

"I get you too," Nico stated, "but damn, screaming like you're being killed scares the crap out of me."

"Sorry." Keela smiled up at him.

"When is Alec gettin' 'ere?" I asked. "I'm starvin'."

"Branna said we're startin' without 'im."

I whistled. "That's not gonna go down well."

Keela, the lads, and I filed out onto the decking of Branna and Ryder's back garden. The smell of barbecue had my mouth watering as I took a seat next to Damien at the newly purchased garden table. Bronagh, who was snuggling her sleeping newborn son, sat across from me. The day after Damien proposed to me and I found out I was pregnant; my best friend went into labour and gave birth to her and Nico's second baby. Nico cried in delight when he was told it was a boy. Bronagh cried with happiness because she was no longer pregnant. My new nephew was called Beau Damien Slater. Beau as in *beau*tiful, not Beau as in bow tie.

Bronagh was clear about the pronunciation, and we were all on board with it rather quickly.

"He's so chunky," I said to Bronagh. "I want to gobble 'im up."

"I know." Bronagh smiled and kissed Beau's head. "I keep

smellin' his head. I *love* that newborn smell."

"Oh, me too," Keela said as she adjusted Enzo's buggy next to her. "I smell his head all the time as well."

"That smell is one of me favourite things." Branna smiled as she fixed the plates that were piled with food on the table. "When I was holdin' Beau yesterday, I could smell it, and I instantly wanted another baby."

Ryder snorted. "It's not like you have long to wait to get another one."

I froze, and so did everyone else. Branna and Ryder laughed.

"You're pregnant?" Bronagh asked, wide-eyed.

"Yeah." She nodded. "I'm five weeks."

I gasped. "Like me! When are you due?"

"The fourth of March."

My jaw dropped because that was *my* due date, and Branna knew it since she was in the room with me and Damien yesterday when we found out at the hospital.

"What the fuck?" Aideen said from our right. "You're both due on the *same day*?"

"Fucking hell." Kane chuckled. "You both apparently had some fun on the *same day*."

Ryder and Damien grinned as congratulations were passed around.

"You're crazy," Bronagh said to her sister. "The twins will be thirteen months when you have this baby … It's just the one baby, right?"

"Yes," Ryder answered on Branna's behalf. "We *triple* checked this time."

"Weren't you gonna wait until the twins were at least one to try for another baby?"

"Yeah," Branna answered me with a nod. "But I forgot to get me latest birth control shot and bam. Pregnant."

"Thank God I'm not the only one who got pregnant because I messed up with birth control."

Everyone laughed.

"Since Alec isn't 'ere, you get the first burger of the summer, Lana."

I rubbed my hands together as Damien put it on my plate. "Come to mama."

"Tell me that in bed tonight," he said, making me grin. "Please."

At that moment, Alec walked out of the kitchen and into the back garden. When his eyes landed on me, he sucked in a startled breath, and Branna looked like she was about to run away as I bit into the first grilled burger of the summer.

"Branna," he all but snarled, his eyes on the burger I held tightly. "What in God's name is this?"

"Um ..." She twitched. "Ye' ... ye' said years ago that she could be your stand-in for first servin's if you were ever absent or late to a meal."

"That privilege was revoked the second she broke my favourite cup!"

"Well, how was I supposed to know that?"

"Because you know me!" Alec stressed.

"I'm sorry, okay?"

He put his back to Branna.

"The betrayal," he said and placed his hand over his chest. "It runs deep."

Nico rolled his eyes at his older brother's dramatics as he bounced Georgie on his knee while everyone else watched the scene unfold with amusement.

"This tastes so good," I hummed. "It's really incredible."

Alec spun around and pointed at me, his hand shaking with obvious anger. "You and me are blood enemies from this day forth, Ryan!"

I had no idea what a blood enemy was, and I didn't care.

"Fine by me, tight arse."

Keela covered up a laugh by covering her mouth with both of her hands while Alec glared holes into my forehead.

"I'll make it up to ye'," Branna said to Alec, slightly gaining his attention. "In fact, I've an offerin' that will make up for this situation right now."

"How?" he demanded, refusing to look at her. "That monster used my cup, then fucking broke it, and now she has eaten the sacred first grilled feast of summer. What can you possibly do to make this better?"

"I've a bigger plate made up with your name on it."

I heard Alec swallow. "How big of a plate are we talking here, Branna?"

Hook, line, and sinker.

"Practically *triple* what everyone else is gettin'."

His four brothers cursed in outrage while Alec turned to face Branna with the biggest smile I had ever seen on his too attractive face.

"I accept your offering and forgive you for feeding Pennywise first."

I rolled my eyes, not offended.

"You'd sell your own child for a plate of dinner."

Alec bared his teeth and hissed at me while holding up his hands and putting his two fingers together to form the symbol of a cross.

"Be gone, demon spawn."

I opened my mouth so he could see the half-eaten burger and then closed it when he pulled a face of disgust.

"You're gross," Alec informed me.

I swallowed then smiled. "Thank you."

"That wasn't a compliment."

"Sure, it was," I beamed. "You've practically just told me ye' love me."

Alec's left eye twitched. "I'm going to shove the rest of that damn burger into your mouth."

I chuckled as I put the burger down and got to my feet.

"I got ye' somethin'," I said as I grabbed the small bag that sat next to the doorway.

"You got *me* something?"

"Yeah," I answered Alec. "Though I'm not sure you deserve it."

He snatched the bag from my grasp before I could finish my sentence. He rustled through it, then removed a box from the inside. Alec sucked in a sharp breath when he realised what I had gotten him.

"You did *not*!"

I most definitely did.

"Alannah!" He beamed as he removed his brand new, extra-large Harry Potter Mischief Manage cup from the box. "It's huge!"

"That's what she said," I answered, making everyone snort.

Everyone except Alec, who walked inside the house, brought his cup over to the kettle and switched it on. I followed him, leaned on the counter, and together, we waited for the kettle to boil. When the switch flipped, Alec popped a tea bag into his new cup, filled it with boiling water, and leaned down and watched the blackness fade, revealing the secret footsteps and popular Harry Potter book quote.

I solemnly swear that I am up to no good.

"I've missed this so much," he said and looked at me. "Thank you."

I nodded. "You're welcome."

"Now." He grinned, his grey eyes shining. "*Never* fucking touch my cup again."

I grinned. "No promises."

"No promises, *Lord Alec*," he corrected.

I scowled. "I *still* think it was a fluke that Tyson barked and ran to find you when Keela's water broke."

"You lost the bet, stick to your terms. You have to call me Lord Alec for one whole month."

"I hate ye' … *Lord Alec*."

Alec beamed. "This is one of the best days of my life. I want you to know that, demon spawn."

I huffed.

"You all need to admit that I'm the baby whisperer *and* the dog

whisperer. Things would just be easier if you accept the gift that is
me. I'm a blessing. I'm practically a modern-day Jesus."

"You can't be a modern-day Jesus." I rolled my eyes. "You only
have fifty followers on Twitter."

Alec grinned. "Jesus only need twelve."

My eye twitched. "Damien?"

"Yeah, freckles?" he called.

"Your brother is comparin' 'imself to Jesus … again."

"Just go with it, freckles." Damien laughed as Alec tugged me
back out to the decking with his new prized Harry Potter cup in the
air for everyone to see. "Just go with it."

"I want to make this *very* clear," Alec said, gaining everyone's
attention. "Alannah is not allowed to touch my cup. Ever. If you see
her drink from it, touch it, or even look at it, then you are to revoke
her tea privileges when she visits your houses. Otherwise, I will
withhold my fine looking redheaded son from you all."

I sucked in a sharp breath, and so did everyone else.

"Sorry, Lana," everyone said in unison.

I understood their betrayal. Enzo was too cute and won over me
any day, but his father, on the other hand, had just ignited a fire
within me.

"War," I told him. "This means *war*."

"Bring it, chicken legs."

"Aren't you glad you're marryin' 'er?" Bronagh asked Damien
as Alec and I continued to glare at one another

"Bee"—Damien laughed—"you have *no* fucking idea."

COMING SEPTEMBER 18TH, 2018

BROTHERS

A Slater Brothers Novel

By L.A. Casey

DOMINIC

PART ONE

CHAPTER ONE

Present day...

When you had five children, sleep was very hard to come by. Sleeping in on the weekends? That was practically unheard of. I was a trier, if anything, so ever since I first became a father fifteen years ago, I attempted, every single weekend, to catch a few extra Zs. My wife, and mainly my know-no-boundries children, made it their personal mission to make sure I didn't.

"Daddy?"

I refused to lift my eyelids as I grumbled, "Go away."

"Come on, Daddy. Get up."

I snored. Loud.

"Daaaaaaddy?"

I groaned but kept my eyes shut, hoping the kid harassing me would give up and leave.

"I know you're fakin' it."

"Go bother your mom," I half pleaded, snuggling into my pillow. "Please."

I felt tiny, soft hands touch my bare back, and that was when the let's-pretend-dad-is-a-drum game started.

"I don't wanna play with a *girl*. I want to play with *you*. You're stronger than Mammy."

I chuckled gruffly before I rolled onto my back, halting the drum game my son had started. I reached up and rubbed my eyes before I opened them and stared at the ceiling of my bedroom. A ceiling that had multiple stickers of stars and moons stuck to it from when Georgie was a baby. I turned my head to the left and came face to face with my actual baby. I reached over, gripped under Axel's armpits, and heaved him onto the bed, making him squeal with laughter. He was the youngest of our five, our last child. My baby. He was spoiled rotten because of this.

"Your mom is plenty strong. Why don't you want to play with her?"

"I'm not talkin' to 'er anymore."

He said this as he sat directly on my chest, making me grunt.

"Why not?"

Axel scowled. "She keeps callin' me a *baby*."

My lips twitched.

"You don't think you're a baby?"

"I just turned *seven*," Axel said, puffing his chest out with pride. "I'm not a baby, Daddy."

I grinned at him. "Your mom doesn't mean anything when she calls you baby, son. It's just a habit from when your brothers and sister were little. She even calls *me* baby now and then … Do you think that *I* look like a baby?"

Axel considered this, then giggled. "You're *definitely* not a baby."

He spoke as he poked at my abdominal muscles. Muscles that at thirty-eight were still tight, toned, and *very* defined. My love for working out never faded as I got older and neither did my wife's adoration for my body, so I made sure to keep everything tight and toned because it made her moan on sight.

I *loved* hearing that woman moan.

I yawned. "Is Mom still in her pjs?"

"Yup," Axel said, popping the P. "She said she's gettin' a shower when ye' wake up."

"I better go downstairs and relieve her then. What do you say?"

Axel looked down at me, a brow raised. "Are ye' goin' to kiss 'er again?"

"Do you not like when I kiss her?"

He shook his head. "She's *my* mammy."

"And she's *my* wife," I countered, grinning.

"I was in 'er belly," Axel deadpanned. "Beat that."

Easy.

"I *put* you in her belly."

He stared down at me. "How?"

I hesitated, wondering if he was too young for the talk that I had given to all my other kids at various ages, but Axel's attention switched to flicking my nipples and laughing when I flinched. He crawled off me when I playfully swatted his hands away, then jumped off the bed and ran out of the room shouting, "I woke 'im up, Ma!"

I shot into an upright position. "You said you wanted to play!"

"I lied," Axel shouted as he reached the stairs. "Mammy said I'd get the *biggest* cookie ever after dinner tonight if I woke ye' up. Sorry … not really, though! Cooookkkiieeee."

I kicked the blankets off my body, before turning to the left and hanging my legs over the bed. I snorted as I heard my wife praise our youngest at the bottom of the stairs for waking me up. I wasn't surprised that she enlisted our kids' help; she always had them scheming when she didn't want to do something. She said it was one of the perks of having children.

"Beau!" Georgie suddenly bellowed. "Give it back or I swear to God I'll—"

"Hey!" I shouted, getting to my feet and walking out to the hallway to see what was going on.

Georgie, my eldest, had Beau, my second eldest, in a chokehold with her arm hooked perfectly around his neck. She had her right leg wrapped around his left to angle his body so she could get a firm grip in a better stance, and he couldn't attempt to break her hold on him without hurting himself in the process. I had taught her how to protect herself and how to hold her own, but she wasn't supposed to practice her self-defence moves on her brothers.

I stared at my firstborn son, and a flashback of his birth suddenly entered my mind.

"He's perfect, baby," I said to my exhausted partner as she cradled our newborn son against her chest. "He's so perfect."

"He looks so much like you, Dominic." Bronagh smiled. "We have a mini me and now a mini you."

"How did we get so lucky?" I asked. "How did I get so lucky?"

Bronagh smiled up at me, so I leaned down, closing the distance between us, and brushed my lips over hers.

"What will we name him?"

"I love the name Beau."

I raised a brow and leaned back. "How do you spell that?"

"B-E-A-U."

"That's pronounced Bo, baby. I like that, though. Let's name him that."

Bronagh blinked. "No, it's pronounced Beau as in beautiful.*"*

"In the States—"

"We aren't in the States." She cut me off with a twitch of her eye. "I like Beau bein' pronounced like the word beautiful. Bo can be his nickname, if you're so pressed about it."

"Okay." I chuckled. "His name is Beau like beautiful, and Bo will be his nickname. I'll inform my brothers of this to avoid your wrath."

Bronagh smiled. "What will his middle name be?"

My heart warmed when I said the name, "Damien."

Bronagh beamed up at me. "Beau Damien Slater. I love it, I love him ... I can't wait for Georgie to see 'im. She's a big sister now."

"Alannah will bring her up when I call," I said. "She'll be with us soon."

Bronagh closed her eyes and snuggled Beau.

"I love our family."

"I love you, *pretty girl."*

"I love you too, fuckface."

"Let him go, Georgie," I said, my mind snapping back to the present.

"He has me phone, Da!"

"Let him *go*," I repeated, sternly. *"Now."*

Georgie gave Beau's neck one last squeeze before she released him and forcefully shoved him to the floor. I folded my arms across my chest and stared down at my only daughter. She placed her hands on her hips and stared right back at me. I looked at my son as he groaned on the floor, then looked back at Georgie.

"Was that really necessary?"

"Yes," she answered without hesitation. "He took me phone without permission, Da."

I looked at Beau. "Why'd you take her phone?"

He groaned as he pushed himself to his feet, then straightened up to his full height. He was fourteen, but he already dwarfed Georgie's five-foot-two frame with his five-foot-eight. When he stood next to her, it always amused me. He was fifteen months younger than she was, and he physically looked down at her. My daughter, however, never let a trivial thing like height stop her when it came to disciplining her brothers or any of her many male cousins. She'd had years of practice on how to harm them when she needed to. Or wanted to.

"I was only messin' with 'er, Da," Beau said before side glancing at his sister. "She's a bleedin' psycho."

Georgie kicked Beau in the shin. He yelped, grabbed his shin with both hands, and hopped around on one foot.

"Bo, give your sister back her phone," I ordered. "And George, stop hitting your brother."

I hoped by using their nicknames, the situation would calm to somehow make it playful, but Georgie's antsy teenage attitude refused to cooperate.

"No promises," she said to me as she snapped her phone out of Beau's outstretched hand. "Next time, I'm breakin' your bloody leg."

She turned and stormed down the hall and into her bedroom, the door clanking shut behind her. Beau shook his head, then his leg, before he lowered his foot to the ground and trained his eyes on me.

"Ye' need to send 'er to a mental institution, Da," he said, his face the picture of seriousness. "She is a bloody nightmare."

I raised a brow. "She wouldn't bother you if you didn't touch her things."

"I wouldn't bother 'er if she didn't annoy the life outta me."

I lifted my hand to my face and pinched the bridge of my nose.

"It's too early to deal with this."

"It's after nine."

I dropped my head. "Exactly. That's early."

Beau snorted as shouting and a bellow from my wife sounded from downstairs.

"Not in this house."

I pointed at my son. "Leave your sister alone. Otherwise, she'll whoop you."

"Only 'cause I won't hit 'er back!"

"I know." I grinned. "When you're bigger and fill out more, she won't be able to grapple you so easily."

"I can't feckin' wait."

"Language."

"Feckin' isn't a curse." Beau rolled his eyes. "And neither is damn or hell."

"The former can slide because it's part of everyone's vocabulary in this country, but if I hear you say the second and third, your ass will be whooped by *me*. Understand?"

"Yes, sir."

"Good." I nodded. "Now, go clean your room. It's Saturday, and you *know* your mom will raise all kinds of hell if she finds it dirty when she makes her rounds."

As I walked down the stairs, Beau asked, "How come you get to say hell and not be whooped?"

"Who is gonna whoop me?"

"You've got a point, Da." Beau paused. "You've got a real good point."

I laughed as I jogged downstairs. A glance into the sitting room revealed Axel lying upside down on the couch as he watched a cartoon on the television. I crossed my arms over my chest and stared at him.

"You're going to give yourself a headache watching the TV like that, Ax."

"No, I won't," he replied, not taking his eyes off the TV. "I always watch it like this."

I had no doubt.

"Just sit up every few minutes; otherwise, the blood will rush to your head."

"Okay, Daddy."

I shook my head in amusement, dropped my arms to my sides, and walked down the hallway and into the kitchen. My eyes found her the second I entered the room. With her back to me as she cooked breakfast, I took a moment to drink her in. In twenty years, nothing about her had changed. Not really, even after five kids. Her body was the same level of perfection it had always been. Small waist, thick thighs, and an ass so fat it still made my knees weak when I looked at it.

Her hair was shorter—it hung just past her shoulders instead of touching her butt—but it was still a beautiful shade of chocolate brown. She had more laugh lines around her eyes, more stretch marks and a slight tummy pouch from having so many babies, but she didn't look thirty-eight years old. She could easily pass as late twenties, and I told her that often because it was true ... not just because it got me laid whenever I said it.

She was tiny, feminine, and was the greatest love of my life, along with my five children. Children *she* gave to me. I glanced down at my ringed finger, smiling at the reminder that we recently celebrated our thirteenth wedding anniversary. We'd been married for thirteen years, but together for twenty, and I couldn't wait to spend fifty more with her, God willing. I couldn't imagine spending my life with anyone else, and I didn't want to, either.

"Good morning, Mrs Slater."

I knew she smiled without having to turn around. I could sense it on her.

"Good mornin', Mr Slater," she replied. "How did ye' sleep?"

"Before or after you woke me up with your mouth on—"

When she spun around and narrowed her bright green eyes at me, my own laughter cut me off.

"Children," she whispered hissed. "They are present."

I glanced to my left, noting my third and fourth sons, Quinn and Griffin, sitting at the kitchen table on the far end of the room, not paying us a lick of attention. I turned my attention back to my wife and grinned.

"They can't hear me."

She gave me a once-over, her eyes lingering on my groin and torso a little too long, allowing naughty thoughts to enter my mind, but like I knew she would, she turned back to face the stove.

"I made you eggs, and I'm workin' on your protein pancakes," she said, rustling the pan to make the pancake flip. "The boys horsed down the first two batches I made, as well as two ten-egg omelettes."

"Q and Griff?"

"Yeah," she answered with a shake of her head. "Axel and Beau had cereal; Georgie hasn't been down to eat yet. Quinn and Griffin are goin' to eat us out of a home all by themselves. I can't believe how much they can put away. They're just as bad as Locke, and that lad never stops eatin'."

"They're growing boys."

Bronagh snorted. "Growin' boys, me arse; they are always feckin' hungry."

"So were my brothers and I growing up." I chuckled. "We still are."

"Oh, I know," my wife answered. "I do the cookin'. I know how much your fat self can gobble up."

I stepped closer to her, pressing my body against hers and sliding my arms around her tiny waist.

"You think I'm fat?" I teased. "My body fat percentage would disagree with you."

"You have the appetite of a fat person and so do your kids. Well, except Georgie, but she *used* to eat just as much." Bronagh shook her head. "I don't know how we afford it. Ye' know, it costs me nearly three hundred and fifty euros a week on *just* food? I don't even shop in Dunnes anymore because it'll easily reach over four hundred in price if I go in there."

I leaned down and kissed her cheek.

"Why are you worrying about this?" I questioned. "I make more than enough to cover our bills. We own the house since Branna signed it over to you, and the cars are brand new since we traded in our others for a steal of a price. We have a fantastic policy on our family health insurance *and* both of our life insurance policies. You set aside money each month to pay our bills on time. You're worrying yourself over nothing."

"I know." She sighed, her body relaxing. "It's just with the football season startin' back up, and the lads all bein' taller with bigger feet, it means we have to buy all new team uniforms and tracksuits, and new football boots, which are over one hundred euros *each* in their sizes, and new clothes since they've no summer clothes that fit. Don't even get me *started* on Georgie's art supplies. She goes through them so fast that we need to replenish every—"

"Sweetheart," I cut Bronagh off. "We have savings for a reason. *This* kind of reason."

She tensed all over again as she placed a large pancake on top of four others next to the large omelette that I assumed was for me.

"Heat the eggs up," she grumbled. "They've been coolin' while

I made the pancakes."

I watched her as she moved around me.

"Bronagh, honey—"

"I'm goin' to get a shower," she cut me off, leaving the room. "I won't be long."

I stared after her, frowning. I had no idea why she was so worried about our finances all of a sudden. Ten years ago, I got a loan from my older brother Kane and bought a broken down old building in the city centre and demolished it. After rebuilding it from the ground up, I opened Slater's 24/7 Fitness. Every month since it opened nine years ago, it'd turned a considerable profit. I was even considering opening a second gym in Tallaght because the main one was doing so well. I paid Kane back and had no debt whatsoever.

Bronagh knew all of this, so I had no idea why she was worrying about paying for our children's sports gear or art supplies. I had enough to buy hundreds of football cleats. Hell, we could buy another house if we wanted to. My instinct was to follow her and find out what was truly bothering her, but over the years, I'd learned that she needed her space when she got upset. Normally, I invaded her space and didn't give her a chance to run away when an argument got her going, but right now, something else was bothering her. I had to time when I chose to talk to her about it.

With a sigh, I turned to my plate of food and put it into the microwave as instructed. While it heated, I went to the refrigerator with the intention of pouring myself a large glass of orange juice, but when I lifted the carton and found it was empty, I scowled and shut the door with a little force before I turned to my sons.

"Which one of you morons put the empty OJ carton back in the refrigerator?"

Quinn and Griffin pointed at one another, but when Quinn scowled and slapped Griffin's hand, Griffin yelped, most likely thinking Quinn was going to pound on him for lying, which I knew he had done.

"Griffin?"

"I'm sorry," he said, his eyes still on his older brother. "I forgot."

"How do you forget the carton is empty when you can feel it's fucking empty?"

Quinn glanced around me, looking for his mom, but when he saw she wasn't there, he kept his mouth shut about my cussing. I rarely cussed in front of my kids, and especially not to them, but sometimes, they irritated the life out of me when they did dumb shit, and it just slipped out. Putting an empty carton of orange juice back into the refrigerator was a dumb shit thing to do.

"I'm sorry, Da."

I sighed. "It's okay. Just don't do it again."

"I won't."

"And I'm sorry for cussing."

Griffin's lips twitched. "It's okay. Just don't do it again."

Quinn laughed but muffled it with his hand while I smirked.

"You'll tattle on me to your mom otherwise?"

"Well, duh, I'm hardly gonna try to *fight* you."

I snorted. "You'll be as big as me someday. You both will."

"In height, yeah, probably, but you work out a lot. I don't think I'd be into that. I'm lazy."

Griffin *was* lazy.

If you gave him the choice to go outside to play and get fresh air, or stay inside and play video games all day, his games would win every single time. He was on the soccer team purely out of parental force. Bronagh and I ran out of ideas to entice him to leave the house, so we had to resort to giving him an ultimatum. He either joined the soccer team or picked a different sport or activity to participate in, or all his gaming consoles, his computer, *and* his phone were going in the trash.

He signed up for the soccer team the next day.

Beau, at fourteen, played for the sixteen and under soccer team, Quinn and Griffin, who were twelve and eleven, played for the under thirteen team, and Axel had just joined the under eight team. Griffin tolerated the soccer team, but damn, the kid was good. Luckily, Beau and Quinn were awesome too, but they lived and breathed the sport. It wasn't punishment to make them go to practice or to games; it was punishment to *stop* them from attending. Axel's team wasn't competitive because of the age group, so each game for him was just for fun, but he loved it.

Then there was Georgie, who was fifteen. My eldest, my only girl ... the only girl out of the twenty-five children my brothers and I have fathered.

Sports were out of the question for her because her passion lay with sketching, painting, and, recently, sculpting. The many years of being in her aunt Alannah's company had rubbed off on her. She started drawing when she was young, and with Alannah's guidance and her own talent, she could draw a lifelike portrait of someone by the time she was thirteen. She loved art; it was her form of self-expression. She attended a local art class on the weekends to gain more experience for the rare time when she wasn't around her aunt. Alannah and Bronagh were joined at the hip but even more so since she started dating my twin brother, Damien, many years ago.

"You're always gonna be lazy if you don't get your head out of the video games you play all the time."

Griffin rolled his eyes and grumbled something under his breath.

"What was that?"

"Nothin', Da," he grunted. "I just don't wanna hear ye' givin' out to me about playin' on me games again. You and Ma always get on me case about it."

"Because you're always on it."

"I joined the football team like ye' both said I had to do," he protested. "Isn't that enough?"

"For now, yeah."

He relaxed, then went back to eating his breakfast.

"What time is your game?"

"Eleven," Quinn and Griffin replied in unison.

"Is Mom taking you guys?"

Quinn's lips twitched. "She said *you* could either take us, or ye' could go and get the shoppin' instead."

I paused. "Grocery shopping?"

Quinn nodded, then smiled at my horrified expression. I *never* did the grocery shopping. The one and only time I'd done it in the past was an utter disaster. I apparently got the wrong brand of half of the groceries on Bronagh's list and forgot the rest. She had to go back to the store and get the correct stuff, which put her in a pissy mood for that entire day. It was a horrible experience from start to finish, and I'd do just about anything to get out of it. My kids and my wife knew that.

"I'm taking you guys to the game."

Griffin snickered. "Thought so."

Quinn chuckled along with him before inhaling one of his pancakes. I joined them at the table with my food, and we talked about school, sports, and girls while we ate. Recently, both boys had taken a mild interest in girls. It was nothing explicit; they had just started to develop crushes now that they no longer found girls gross.

"Griffin's got two girlfriends," Quinn announced as we all finished our food. "They fight over 'im."

Griffin's cheeks burned. "Shut *up*, Q!"

I frowned at Griffin. "Is that true, Griff?"

"No," he insisted. "They just like me or somethin'. They follow me around at school and get mad when I talk to one girl and not the other. They aren't me girlfriends, though. I don't have one, let alone *two*."

"Good," I said, firmly. "That's disrespectful to play two girls like that."

"I know." Griffin nodded. "We have to be nice to girls and treat them like we'd want a lad to treat Georgie, or you to treat Mom. I remember our talk."

"You said Mom." Quinn snickered.

Griffin scowled at him. "It's only 'cause I was talkin' to Da!

You say words like 'im sometimes, too."

I rolled my eyes.

"It's not a bad thing to say words how I say them. I know you guys are Irish, but you're American, too. That's half of my blood flowing through your veins, and I told you it's important to know your heritage."

"Ma said we don't really have an American heritage 'cause the country was stolen like *forever* ago."

I paused. "Okay, that is true but—"

"We're Irish, but because of you, we have American heritage," Quinn cut me off. "We *know*. Please don't tell us about it again. I feel like we're in school when you do."

I had to keep from smiling. He looked pained at the thought of me lecturing him about my homeland.

"Put your dishes in the dishwasher and go upstairs and clean your rooms," I said. "Mom won't let you go to your game if you don't do your chores."

Griffin perked up at the prospect of getting out of a soccer game, so I added, "She'll also confiscate your Xbox, desktop, and phone if she has to keep you home from soccer."

Griffin grunted as he got to his feet. "She's evil."

I snorted as they left the room after taking care of their dishes and mine. I relaxed at the table for a moment, then turned my head when Georgie entered the room, fully dressed in jeans, ankle boots, and a sweater.

"You'll be too warm wearing a sweater and boots today, baby. It's warm outside."

Georgie glanced at me and snorted.

"I'm always freezin', Da. There's no such thing as too hot for me. Not in this country, anyway."

My lips quirked as she moved around the kitchen, cleaning up after Bronagh had made everyone breakfast. That was one of Georgie's chores; she preferred cleaning the kitchen to the bathrooms. The boys would flip a coin to see who got stuck with toilet duty.

"What are you doing today, sweetheart?"

"I have class at the centre at half ten," she answered. "Auntie Alannah is collectin' me on 'er way. Alex and Joey are comin' with me."

"And here I thought you would come to the boys' game with me to keep me company."

The look of horror Georgie shot my way cracked me up. Her lips twitched when she realised I was teasing her.

"Will ye' go and get dressed?" she asked, her brow wrinkled. "You're too old to be walkin' around in your boxers like the lads."

"Too old?" I repeated in outrage. "I'm thirty-eight, you little shit."

Georgie smirked. "That's only two years away from forty."

I scowled. "Evil child."

"I'm gonna be twenty in five years, does that make you feel worse?"

Pain clutched at my chest.

"Yes," I answered, rubbing the spot. "It does. You're my baby."

"D'ye hear that, Axel?" Georgie hollered. "Daddy just called me a *baby*!"

I heard movement, then quick paced little footsteps as my youngest son barrelled into the room, wrapping his arms around Georgie's hips when he crashed into her, making her laugh.

"I *told* ye'!" Axel said to her. "I told ye' they think we're all babies."

"Ye' did." Georgie nodded down at him. "I think Mammy and Daddy are goin' crazy."

"*Super* crazy!"

"Hey," I teased. "You're *all* my babies."

"He's lost his mind," Axel said with a shake of his head. "We should put 'im in the old people's home ye' said he and Mammy are gonna go to someday."

141

My jaw dropped, and Georgie burst into laughter.

"Ye' aren't supposed to *tell* them what I said," she tittered, hugging her brother to her side. "They get upset when we call them old."

"Ohhh." Axel nodded. "It's a secret."

"A *super* secret."

Everything was super to Axel when it was being stressed.

"A *super* secret." He nodded and looked like he accepted a mission of some kind. "I got it."

"A nursing home?" I blinked at my daughter. "Really?"

She smiled wide, and it warmed my heart.

She was the picture of her mother, and apart from my dimples, no one would ever guess she was my daughter. Bronagh got all the genetic rights to our firstborn; she got those rights with Quinn, too. He was the only one of my sons who resembled his mother more than me. He had her green eyes, her perfect complexion, her nose, her mouth. Everything. The rest of our boys got my genetics, which meant they looked the Slater part. Beau was the spitting image of Damien's firstborn son, and since they were close in age, people often thought they were twins, which amused them greatly.

"I'm only teasin'," Georgie assured me with a wink. "I'd never put you in an old folk's home. I wouldn't be able to carry ye'."

I snorted. "Watch your brother while I go shower."

Georgie saluted me, then ducked out of my reach with Axel, both screaming with laughter when I fake dived for them. A big smile stretched across my face as I left the room and jogged upstairs. I heard blaring music coming from the attic that was converted into a bedroom a few years before Axel was born. It was Beau's room, and ever since he hit his teenage years, I was considering soundproofing the damn thing because Beau only understood one volume, and that was *loud*.

"Beau!" I yelled and banged on the rail of the spiral stairs that led up to his room. "Boy, you better answer me."

The music switched off, and the door to his room opened ever so slightly.

"What, Da?"

"Turn that garbage *down!*" I warned. "We have neighbours, you know?"

"Sorry," Beau said, popping his head out just enough for me to see he was red faced and sweating. "I'll keep it low."

His door clicked then, and just as I was about to walk up the stairs to see what he was doing, I paused. The last time I walked into his room unannounced, I got an eyeful of my teenager jerking off like there was no tomorrow. He couldn't look me in the eye for a week after that happened, and since it only occurred a few months ago, I had to keep boundaries and respect his privacy. I remembered what it was like to be fourteen and hormonal. You got wood from something as simple as sniffing fucking flowers.

The only difference between me and my son was that I didn't have to jerk off. I had paid escorts to take care of my needs. I was sure that was a perk from my past life that Beau would desperately love to avail of. With a grin, I shook my head and walked into my bedroom. I glanced at the closed bathroom door and heard the shower running. I quickly closed the bedroom door, kicked off my boxers, and tiptoed my way into the bathroom.

I hadn't had shower sex with my wife in *months*, and there was no way I was going to miss the opportunity of loving her while she was dripping wet. When I stepped into the room, steam slapped me in the face. I could barely see a thing, and that was typical Bronagh. She had to have her shower water run so damn hot before she'd even consider stepping under the spray. The room was like our own personal sauna.

"Hey, mama."

Bronagh jumped when I entered the shower behind her, but she didn't spin to face me.

"You're so predictable," she said with a snort. "I knew ye'd come up 'ere."

I reached out and palmed her ass when I was close enough to do so.

"Can you blame me?" I asked, leaning down and swiping my tongue over her earlobe. "Your ass makes my cock ache."

"After all this time?" She wiggled her ass against me. "I've still got it, fuckface."

My lips twitched as I looked down and watched as I shifted my hips and began to slowly thrust back and forth. My cock, snugly between Bronagh's ass cheeks, felt like heaven. I bit down on my lower lip when she clenched her cheeks together, and it sent a wave of bliss riveting straight to my balls.

"Fu...*ck*."

"You want me arse?"

I pressed my mouth against Bronagh's sopping wet hair.

"*Yes*," I rasped. "Yes, please, baby."

She rarely let me fuck her ass, so when she did, it felt like all my Christmases came at once.

"Get me ready."

Those words sent blood rushing to my already throbbing cock.

I dropped to my knees behind her, leaning forward and biting her ass, making her suck in a sharp breath, then laugh.

"Bastard."

I smiled as I slid my tongue over the flesh I bit. Without warning, I spread her wide and plunged my tongue into her asshole. Bronagh's hands flattened against the tiled walls. My arm wrapped around her, flattening against her stomach in an effort to support her in case she slipped and fell. I groaned when Bronagh's hand ran over mine before she pushed it down to her pussy, showing me what she wanted me to do. My fingers found her clit and hearing the first long moan come from her caused my balls to tighten.

I fucking *loved* when she moaned.

I tongued her asshole and played with her clit until her body trembled. When I stood, I fisted my cock and pumped it twice before I aligned the head with Bronagh's body. I used my left hand to spread her, and when I slowly thrust my hips forward, my eyes fluttered shut. The tightness, the heat, the pulsing of my wife's muscles.

It was an ecstasy that only she could give me. I forced my eyes open so I could watch as my cock slipped inside her mag-fucking-nificent ass, and as always, I couldn't stop my eyes from rolling to the back of my head as pleasure licked at me.

"Dominic," Bronagh whispered. "Fuck."

Fuck was right.

"Baby," I lowly groaned. "You always feel so perfect."

"Easy," she whispered. "Go *easy*."

I had to go easy with her. No matter how many times I fucked her ass, I always had to be very gentle with her in the beginning until she was stretched and used to the sensation of being so full. She came harder when I started out easier, so I took my time thrusting in and out of her body. I brought my mouth to her neck and kissed her skin until her head fell back against my chest.

"Mine," I grunted as I scraped my teeth over her skin. "Everything about you is *mine*. I'm going to fuck you into ecstasy, baby."

"Yes," she replied, starting to push back against my body. "Fuck. Yes."

Bronagh wildly bucked back against me, giving me just as good as I was giving her. The only sounds that could be heard were our laboured breathing, the slapping of skin on skin, and the occasional grunt or groan that neither of us could contain. I picked up my pace and fucked my wife harder. When she played with her clit and groaned, the sound went straight to my balls, and I bucked into her harder, faster, deeper. When she sucked in a sharp breath, held it and went still as I fucked her, I knew she was coming. I hissed when her asshole tightened around me as her muscles contracted.

"Good girl," I praised, running my tongue over her shoulder. "Fuck. You feel so good."

Now that she had come, I had to chase down my own orgasm because in the back of my mind I knew that at any moment, one of the kids was going to call us and put an indefinite pause on our alone time. It took another thirty seconds, but when my balls drew up tight and a shiver danced the length of my spine, I knew I was about to come. My lips parted and deep groans filled the room as the first spurt shot free. I hissed when Bronagh's muscles contracted a couples of times and acted like a vacuum, sucking the cum out of my cock.

"Baby!"

She chuckled in response.

"I fucking *love* you," I panted, slapping her ass for good measure. "You continue to ruin me."

Bronagh grunted against the wall. "Ye've just about fucked me into a coma, big man."

I laughed as I slipped out of her body. I spent a few minutes catering to her. I washed her hair and body because not only did I love doing it, but *she* loved me doing it.

"Are you going to tell me what got you upset in the kitchen earlier?"

She turned to face me, looked up at me, and my heart thumped against my chest. She was beautiful, so painfully beautiful that I could never get enough of her. This woman had my heart, body, and soul. One look from those big green eyes, and I was completely at her mercy.

"I don't even know what me problem is," she answered with a sigh. "Sometimes, I just realise we have such a big family, and I'm terrified if we suddenly can't provide for them anymore."

"Bronagh."

"You're the one who makes the money, Dominic," she cut me off. "I just … I just—"

"You just take care of everyone and everything else," I finished. "Sweetheart, you are the heart of this family. Without you, there is nothing. You know that."

When her eyes glazed over with tears, I leaned down and kissed her until she relaxed against me.

"Alannah pays you too. You've been working with her for years. You contribute financially as well as me."

She sighed but didn't disagree with me.

"No more worrying," I murmured against her lips. "Okay?"

She nodded. "Okay."

"I love you."

She hummed. "I love ye', too."

I jumped when her nails ran over my softening cock, and it made her laugh as I backed out of the shower with a smirk in place.

"Same time tomorrow?"

Bronagh snorted. "If I can sit down by then, we'll see."

I left our bathroom with a shit-eating grin on my face. I dried myself off, changed into clean boxer shorts, and just as I was about to grab some pants, I thought I heard voices in the hallway. I ventured outside to investigate, and the second I left the room, gasps and giggles could be heard, as well as a horrified, "*Da!*"

Georgie was clearly heading towards her bedroom with two of her friends in tow, Alexandra and Joanne aka Alex and Joey. I had known both girls since they were in kindergarten with my daughter, so seeing them stare at me without blinking freaked me out. I looked down at my boxer briefs then back up to my child's teenage friends, and I think, for the first time in years, I felt myself blush.

"Hi, girls." I smiled as I reached out to grab a towel hanging over the stair rail and wrapped it tightly around my hips. "How are you, ladies?"

"I'm doin' *real* good, Mr. Slater," Joey replied with a brow raised and her teeth sinking into her lower lip. "Real good, sir."

Alex giggled and Joey stared at me without blinking while Georgie looked mortified if her burning face was any indication.

"Can you please put some clothes on?" she pleaded. "*Please.*"

I bobbed my head and sprung back into my bedroom and closed the door behind me before anyone could speak another word. Bronagh was in the middle of putting a bra on. She already had socks and panties on, and when she saw me, she raised her brows.

"Alex and Joey just saw me in my boxers." I cringed. "I think Joey licked her lips, too."

Bronagh grinned. "Is Georgie red faced?"

"Yeah," I answered. "She'll be complaining about this for the next week."

My wife giggled as she pulled on a pair of jeans, and she playfully rolled her eyes when she found my eyes glued to her as she got dressed. I grinned, not ashamed in the least to be caught ogling her. I watched her as often as I could, and she and everyone else knew it. My kids weren't bothered by it because seeing me being constantly affectionate to their mother was all they ever knew. I think if I stopped showing that affection, they would find it weird.

"You'll have to apologise to Georgie," Bronagh said as she put on her socks. "She'll be a nightmare otherwise."

I pulled on jeans, socks, and a t-shirt.

"I'll catch her before she goes to the centre with the girls."

"I'm bringin' Axel shoppin' with me, so you just have Quinn and Griffin to bring to their game. Their game is a home game, so it's just down to the pitches for you. I wanna stop off at Skechers and get Axel new runners; his last two pairs were ruined from all the climbin' he does at Gravity with you."

I smiled. "He loves it."

"His runners don't."

I walked over, smacked her ass, grabbed her face, and kissed her like I meant it. When I pulled away, my wife swayed into me just like she did when we were teenagers.

"What was that for?"

"Because I felt like kissing you."

She opened her eyes and smiled up at me.

"You're so beautiful."

"Speakin' of beautiful." She smiled. "Why were Beau and Georgie fightin' earlier?"

"He took her phone; she retaliated."

"That lad constantly tries to find ways to annoy 'er."

"He loves her … loves to piss her off, too."

Bronagh chuckled as I kissed her cheek and left the room. I glanced over the stair rail and saw Alex and Joey descending the

stairs with my daughter nowhere in sight. I made my way to her bedroom, and when I entered the room, I froze in the doorway.

"What the *hell* are you wearing, Georgie Slater?"

She spun to face me, and when I saw her bare stomach, my heart
stopped.

"You were right ab-about it bein' hot out," she stammered. "I
was just changin' into somethin' … cooler."

"Cooler?" I blinked. "You're naked."

"Da, *please.*" She frowned. "I'm not naked. It's a crop top and a
skirt."

Two things she had never worn before. Ever.

"Naked," I repeated. "You aren't leaving the house in *that.*"

I ran from her room to mine, grabbed a t-shirt that I made as a
joke the year before, and rushed back to my daughter's room. I
pushed it at her and waited outside as she changed into it. When I
heard her screech, I felt deeply satisfied with myself.

"Daddy!"

"Don't 'daddy' me," I warned as I re-entered the room. "If you
won't dress yourself correctly, then *I'll* do it for you."

My child almost snarled at me. "This will put me at the *top* of
the loser list, Da! No lad will ever look in me direction if ye' make
me wear this!"

Fireworks went off in my mind at her words.

"You're never taking it off."

Georgie stomped her foot on the ground and turned her back to
me. She opened her mouth and shouted, "Ma!"

I listened for Bronagh and smiled when I heard her walk towards our daughter's room humming a song.

"What is it, Georgie?"

"Da is ruinin' me entire life, and he's *happy* about it."

I was *very* happy about it.

Bronagh entered the room on a tired sigh, but when her gorgeous eyes fell to the t-shirt Georgie had on, she laughed with glee.
Our less than impressed teenager screeched. "It's *not* funny! I'll be

slagged to the high heavens if I have to wear this, Ma.”

Bronagh folded her arms over her chest. “I thought ye’ didn’t care what people thought of ye’?”

Georgie shifted her stance. “I don’t.”

My wife raised a brow. “Then what’s the problem?”

Georgie pointed at her shirt and read the words printed in black.

“This is my dad. He will do to you what you do to me. It’s even worse with the stupid picture of da without his shirt on under the writin’.”

“That’s a nice picture.” I frowned. “Don’t be mean.”

She refused to look at me. Instead, she focused on Bronagh. “I’d sooner walk around school in me *bra* in front of every lad in sixth year than wear this t-shirt, Ma.”

My child just described an actual nightmare of mine.

“Do you want me to have your cousins flank you all day at school on Monday?” I growled. “Because I’ll call them right now and arrange it.”

My stubborn child scoffed. “Go for it.”

She challenged me, and she was old enough to know never to do that.

“Fine,” I said and took out my phone.

“Fine,” Georgie quipped.

I dialled Jax’s number and placed my phone to my ear.

“What’s up, unc?” he answered on the third ring.

“I need a favour, kid.”

I heard a female giggle, then a pained groaned from my nephew. “I’m kind of busy, unc. Can this wait?”

I shook my head as a grin crept its way onto my face.

“It’s about Georgie.”

I heard Jax instantly hush who was giggling.

“Is she okay?” he asked, his focus fully on our conversation and not the girl he was with.

“She is,” I said then growled, “but she is threatening to wear *just* her bra to school.”

150

"She is threatenin' to *what*?" Jax all but roared. "Is she there with ye'?"

"She is."

"Put 'er on the phone," he demanded. "Now."

He was Kane's kid; there was no doubt about it. I tapped my phone on Georgie's shoulder and held it out to her when she turned to me. She looked at the phone for a moment, and I saw her tough girl act begin to crack. She covered up her near slip, took the phone, and pressed it to her ear.

"What do ye' want, Jax?" she asked, though her tone wasn't as stern as before.

I looked at Bronagh when Jax's voice bellowed through the receiver of my phone. She grinned, and I shook my head. She was enjoying this just as much as I was.

"No!" Georgie suddenly bellowed. "If ye' do that, I'll make sure Daisy Mars *never* looks at ye' again." She gasped at Jax's response. "Ye' wouldn't dare."

"I would," I heard Jax threaten.

"Go ahead then," Georgie angrily spat and hung up on Jax before turning and tossing my phone back to me.

"Can ye' both leave, please?" she asked. "I want to be on me own."

I opened my mouth to ignore her and continue our discussion, but when a soft hand touched my elbow, I turned my attention from my daughter to my wife.

"Come on," Bronagh said. "Leave 'er be."

I had to be tugged out of the room and down the stairs.

"Georgie will be down in a few minutes," Bronagh said to Alex and Joey who were in the sitting room with Axel and Beau keeping them company. Beau, whose focus was on Joey, didn't even notice that his mother spoke. He was too focused on his sister's friend, and it made me snort.

Twenty minutes after our argument, Georgie, who was correctly dressed, left with her friends and went to the community centre when

Alannah pulled up outside to collect them. Bronagh took Axel with her when she went shopping, and Beau accompanied me to the boys' soccer game. We didn't get home until after four p.m. After soccer, I took the boys to lunch, then to see the new Marvel movie. When I stepped foot into my house, it sounded like World War III had erupted.

Jax was in the house, and he and Georgie were knee-deep in an argument in the kitchen. I pushed passed my kids and jogged into the room. My wife was leaned against the sink, pinching the bridge of her nose. I looked at my firstborn nephew and my firstborn child, who were glaring daggers at each other. When my nephew caught sight of me, a deadly grin spread across his face.

"Uncle Nico," Jax said, turning his attention back to his cousin. "Georgie has a boyfriend ... and he's a *Collins*!"

Those were the words that I knew deep in my soul would finally be the reason I ended up in prison.

ACKNOWLEDGEMENTS

Annnndddd another one bites the dust. I had so much fun writing *ALANNAH*, but was also freaked out when I came to the end of it because it means I'm one book closer to the *Slater Brothers* series ending … until the two spin off series that they'll all feature in begin, of course. I have my team of helpers that made this novella a reality and without them, I'd just have a bunch of jumbled misspelled words.

Editing4Indies—Jenny, thank you for all the hard work you do on my manuscripts to make them reading ready.

Nicola Rhead—Thank you for always being on call to proofread.

JT Formatting—Jules, thank you for always making the interior of my books look pretty.

Mark Gottlieb—Thank you for being a fantastic agent.

Mayhem Cover Creations—LJ, thank you so much for yet *another* beautiful cover.

Thank you to every single one of my readers for your ongoing support, I love your love for the Slater family <3

ABOUT THE AUTHOR

L.A. Casey is a *New York Times* and *USA Today* best-selling author who juggles her time between her mini-me and writing. She was born, raised and currently resides in Dublin, Ireland. She enjoys chatting with her readers, who love her humour and Irish accent as much as her books.

Casey's first book, *DOMINIC*, was independently published in 2014 and became an instant success on Amazon. She is both traditionally and independently published and is represented by Mark Gottlieb from Trident Media Group.

To read more about this author,
visit her website at www.lacaseyauthor.com

ALSO BY L.A. CASEY

Slater Brothers series:
DOMINIC
BRONAGH
ALEC
KEELA
KANE
AIDEEN
RYDER
BRANNA
DAMIEN

Maji series
OUT OF THE ASHES

Standalone novels
FROZEN
UNTIL HARRY

Made in the USA
Middletown, DE
27 July 2018